W9-AXO-417

JULIE'S WOLF PACK

ALSO BY JEAN CRAIGHEAD GEORGE

Acorn Pancakes, Dandelion Salad,
and 38 Other Wild Recipes

Animals Who Have Won Our Hearts

The Case of the Missing Cutthroats
An Ecological Mystery

The Cry of the Crow

Dear Rebecca, Winter Is Here

Everglades

The Fire Bug Connection
An Ecological Mystery

Going to the Sun

The Grizzly Bear with the Golden Ears

Julie

Julie of the Wolves

Look to the North
A Wolf Pup Diary

The Missing 'Gator of Gumbo Limbo
An Ecological Mystery

The Moon of the Alligators

The Moon of the Bears

The Moon of the Chickarees

The Moon of the Deer

The Moon of the Fox Pups

The Moon of the Gray Wolves

The Moon of the Moles

The Moon of the Monarch Butterflies

The Moon of the Mountain Lions

The Moon of the Owls

The Moon of the Salamanders

The Moon of the Wild Pigs

The Moon of the Winter Bird

One Day in the Alpine Tundra

One Day in the Desert

One Day in the Prairie

One Day in the Tropical Rain Forest

One Day in the Woods

Shark Beneath the Reef

The Summer of the Falcon

The Talking Earth

The Tarantula in My Purse

There's an Owl in the Shower

Water Sky

Who Really Killed Cock Robin?
An Ecological Mystery

The Wounded Wolf

HARPERCOLLINS*PUBLISHERS*

JEAN CRAIGHEAD GEORGE

Julie's Wolf Pack

ILLUSTRATED BY WENDELL MINOR

Library of Congress Cataloging-in-Publication Data

George, Jean Craighead, date

Julie's wolf pack / Jean Craighead George ; illustrated by Wendell Minor.

p.   cm.

Summary: Continues the story of Julie and her wolves in which Kapu must protect his pack from
famine and disease while uniting it under his new leadership.

ISBN 0-06-027406-9. — ISBN 0-06-027407-7 (lib. bdg.)

I. Wolves—Juvenile fiction. [1. Wolves—Fiction.   2. Survival—Fiction.
3. Leadership—Fiction.]   I. Minor, Wendell, ill.   II. Title.

PZ10.3.G316Ju   1997   96-54858

[Fic]—dc21   CIP

                                                                       AC

Typography by Wendell Minor and Al Cetta

1   2   3   4   5   6   7   8   9   10

❖

First Edition

To Luke and Sam,
my grandsons of Barrow, Alaska,
friends of the wolves, whales, foxes, owls,
and the Iñupiat Eskimos

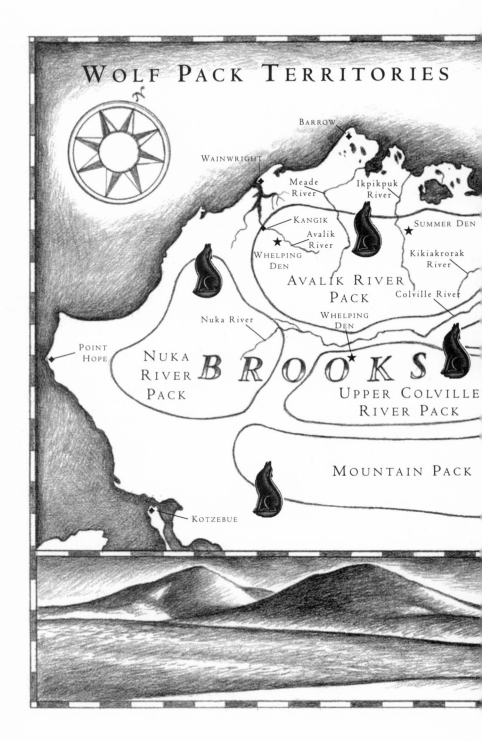

JULIE'S WOLF PACK
YEAR BY YEAR

YEAR ONE
Parents/Alpha Male and Female	Amaroq, Silver
Beta	Nails
Offspring	Kapu, Zing, Zit, Zat, Sister
Other	Jello

YEAR TWO
Parents/Alpha Male and Female	Kapu, Aaka
Beta	Zing
Offspring	Sweet Fur Amy
Special Event	Julie's half brother, Amaroq, is born

YEAR THREE
Parents	Raw Bones, Silver
Offspring	Nutik, Uqaq
Alpha Male and Female	Kapu, Aaka
Beta	Zing
Others	Sweet Fur Amy, Storm Call, Lichen, Ice Blink

YEAR FOUR
Parents/Alpha Male and Female	Kapu, Aaka
Beta	Zing
Offspring	Cotton Grass, Long Face, Grappler, Smiler, White Toes, Black Lips, Nameless Moonlight
Others	Sweet Fur Amy, Raw Bones, Uqaq, Storm Call, Lichen, Wind Voice

YEAR FIVE

Parents	Wind Voice, Uqaq
Offspring	Big Ears, Owl Feathers, Bird Egg
Others	Zing, Aaka, Raw Bones, Lichen, Storm Call, Sweet Fur Amy, Cotton Grass, Long Face

YEAR SIX

Parents	Storm Call, Sweet Fur Amy
Offspring	Six (unnamed)
Others	Aaka, Zing, Lichen, Wind Voice, Uqaq, Big Ears, Owl Feathers, Bird Egg, Cotton Grass, Long Face

OTHER PACKS

LOWER COLVILLE RIVER PACK

Alpha Male	Storm Alarm
Alpha Female	Star Gentian
Offspring	Aaka

NUKA RIVER PACK

Alpha Male	Low Wind
Alpha Female	Moon Seeker

PHILIP SMITH MOUNTAIN PACK

Alpha Male	Sedge Ears
Alpha Female	Alder Whisper

MOUNTAIN PACK

Alpha Male	Snow Driver
Alpha Female	Cloud Berry

CONTENTS

PART I
KAPU, THE ALPHA
I

PART II
ICE BLINK, THE STRANGER
55

PART III
SWEET FUR AMY,
THE NEW ALPHA
153

PART I

KAPU,
THE ALPHA

*T*he wolves of the Avalik River ran in and out among the musk oxen. Their ruffs rippled like banners. Ice crystals danced up from their feet. The pack swirled like a twist of wind-blown snow. Their yellow eyes flashed and dimmed in the coming and going of the ice mist. Like the snow, they made no sound.

The musk oxen stopped and stared at the enemy. Then they lowered their shaggy heads and pawed down to the new grass growing under the snow. Their breath rose in steamy clouds and froze on their brows.

Kapu, the young leader of the wolf pack, reared on his hind legs, leaped to point the way, and led his clan to a turquoise-blue rise on the treeless Arctic tundra.

He carried himself proudly, with his chest forward and his head high. His black fur was brushed to a shine by the wind. His body was strongly muscled.

He was the leader of the wolf pack that had saved the life of the young Eskimo girl, Miyax—whose English name was Julie Edwards—when she was lost on the Arctic tundra. She, in turn, had saved them by leading them to a new food source during the great caribou famine. The Yupik and Iñupiat Eskimos of Kangik called them "Julie's wolf pack."

Kapu was keenly aware of Julie. She was not far away. He whisked his tail. She had read his message to the oxen, for she was no longer afraid that he would kill one. The villagers collected the wool from these sturdy animals to weave into light, warm clothing, and they zealously protected them.

"We are not hunting you," Kapu had said to the oxen with his body movements. "We chase you for the joy of it. We are wolves of the caribou."

Kapu and his followers were having fun. The shaggy herd deciphered this and returned to their grazing. Julie deciphered it and told her father, Kapugen. He chuckled and slipped his arm around her shoulders. The two walked quietly home.

Kapu wagged his tail. Chasing the oxen was a fine wolf joke. His rime-gray mate, Aaka, playfully spanked the ground with her forepaws, her rear end in the air. Zing—the beta, or second in command— enjoyed the joke even more than Kapu. His breathing came faster, and the pupils of his eyes enlarged ever so slightly. He smiled by lifting his lips from his glistening teeth. Pearly-white Silver, Kapu's mother, and her ill-tempered new mate, Raw Bones, also smiled. But Amy, Kapu's night-black daughter, did not get the joke. She was not old enough to know that her pack preferred caribou to musk oxen. Nor did she know that some packs harvest only deer and ignore moose, or harvest moose and caribou and ignore deer. Others take elk; a few take musk oxen. When the Avalik River Pack had a choice, they were wolves of the caribou. Wolves have their cultures.

The adolescent Amy studied the curled horns and bony brows of the musk oxen, then looked at her regal father. If he thought the chase was fun, then she did, too. She wagged her tail.

Amy could not possibly know that her pack were caribou wolves. She had been born in a caribou famine. These big Arctic deer had failed to come to Avalik territory for many years. The pack had taken what food they could find—a musk ox killed by a grizzly bear, rabbits, lemmings. Late in the fall they were able to add an occasional moose to their diet, but by March of her first year Amy's pack was starving again. The moose were gone. The wolves grew thin. They tired easily. When the breeding season arrived that month, her parents did not mate. Aaka, her mother, was undernourished. There had not been enough food for her to develop healthy puppies.

The rangy, self-important Raw Bones knew well that the pack had not had enough to eat for years. Nevertheless, he approached Silver to start their family. Kapu rushed to him. Hair rising on his back, ears erect and pointed forward, Kapu talked to him in the wolf language of posturing. Then he lifted his head above him and rumbled a dark authoritative growl that said plainly, "No pups." It is inherent in the leader of the wolf pack that he uses his judgment and makes such a decision. Raw Bones ignored him. He stepped closer to Silver.

Kapu bared his teeth and drew the corners of his mouth forward. His forehead wrinkled.

Raw Bones challenged this reprimand with a jaw snap. Kapu grabbed the back of his neck but did not clamp down with his bone-crushing jaws. He did not need to. He was saying, "I am the leader. No pups." Raw Bones drew his ears back and close to his head. He pulled his tail between his legs and lowered his body. This posture said, "You are the leader. I submit to you."

Obediently Raw Bones slunk off to the edge of the pack in the manner of a chastised wolf citizen.

But he did not mean it.

He glanced back to see if Kapu was looking at him. If not, he would sneak-attack him. Kapu was looking. He displayed one canine tooth. It shone lethal white against the black of his lips. "Don't dare," it said. Raw Bones lay down. Rumbling sounds of peevishness rolled in his chest. He did not like being dominated, especially by a younger male.

Kapu did not completely relax. Raw Bones was his rival. He wanted to be leader of the Avaliks, Kapu's pack. He had been alpha male wolf of the Upper Colville River Pack for many years. Then the famine struck. One by one the members of his pack starved to death until he was the only one left alive. When his new mate, Silver, joined him, they survived on rabbits and other small mammals and waited for the famine to end and the feasting to begin. Feast and famine are the natural rhythm of the Arctic tundra. The caribou eat themselves out of grasses and moss and move to greener lands. The wolves adjust. Many die. The alpha males and females have few or no pups. Then time heals. Without the caribou to crop them, the grasses and mosses spring up in abundance. The caribou return. The wolves feast and have pups again. This has been the rhythm of nature for the past 500,000 years.

Raw Bones and Silver waited for the cycle to end by sleeping long hours to conserve energy. They were curled tightly, saving body heat, when the Avaliks arrived at the border of their own property across the river. Between Kapu's and Raw Bones's territories was a broad corridor into which neither pack would go. It was the no-wolf zone, an area fenced off with howls and scent marks to keep wolf packs from fighting and killing each other.

Silver heard a wolf voice beyond the no-wolf zone. She lifted her head. Kapu, her son, was calling, "Come hunt with us," communicating in the wolf language of song.

She jumped up, eager to join him. Relatives can cross the no-wolf zone when invited. She trotted toward the river. Raw Bones held back. He had been trained all his life not to enter these corridors. Adolescents leaving home to look for a new pack, and lone wolves, can hide in them, but not leaders. Not Raw Bones.

Yet he had heard Kapu's invitation. Invitations are important in wolf protocol. He arose. A raging hunger and the scent knowledge that Kapu was Silver's son urged him slowly forward.

Silver took a deep draft of air. The perfume of Willow Pup Julie was on it. She wagged her tail. The human cub who had joined her family long ago was coming her way.

Willow Pup Julie appeared among the knobby alder trees. She carried Kapu's invitation in the odors on her clothes. Silver pranced a wolf dance of survival. By joining the Avaliks, she would live. She ran to the river. Raw Bones was reluctant but understood what he must do. Head down, he skirted Willow Pup and splashed into the river behind Silver. They crossed to the forbidden land.

The packs met. Stiff-legged, nervous, they greeted each other with mouth sniffs and brief tail whisks. All tails curved downward and cricked in suspicion, then each hung loose and relaxed to tell the other wolves they would cooperate and hunt together. Antlered animals with their sharp hoofs are violent prey. The more wolves, the better.

But it was not that simple. There can be but one alpha male and one alpha female leading a pack. Kapu and Raw Bones snapped at each other, testing to see which it would be. They were both leaders. The battle for rank began as they lifted their tails. Then each inhaled the other's scent and learned of his health, vigor, and dominance. Finally each growled his lowest note. Raw Bones was older. This gave him the advantage. He raised his head above

Kapu's to say he was boss. Kapu would not tolerate it. He threw Raw Bones to the ground. Raw Bones quickly got to his feet. Kapu lifted his head above Raw Bones's. Both wrinkled their brows and curled back their black lips to show gleaming white fangs. Growling, they threatened each other. Raw Bones tried to get his paw on Kapu's back, but Kapu kept his head and chest above him. He snarled deep and low. With that the battle was over. Not a drop of blood was spilled. Kapu had won.

This was an important victory for the young wolf leader. Upon the death of his father, Amaroq, he had taken over the leadership of the pack. The death of an alpha male wolf is a tragedy, like the death of a nation's president. For the wolves it takes many years to make a leader as strong and knowledgeable as Amaroq had been. Kapu did not have time to develop with Raw Bones in his pack. To survive, he had to be dominant now. He had the fearlessness and initiative of an alpha, but he was young. That is a disadvantage when confronted with an older wolf. By sheer bravado, by snarling and growling and keeping his head above Raw Bones's, Kapu had held on to his rank as alpha male wolf of the Avaliks.

Raw Bones did not like it. He would try again.

Leadership settled for the moment, the six wolves

worked together that early-autumn season hunting the moose that had been protected for years in the no-wolf zone. At first they fared well; then the moose became scarce. Grizzlies and human hunters were also harvesting them.

The famine went on. The caribou did not migrate south through Avalik land in the late fall. The wolves lost weight and vigor.

In March, the breeding month, Kapu made the decision for himself and Aaka as well as for Silver and Raw Bones not to have pups.

Many sleeps later, his sensitive ears picked up the sounds he had been waiting for: the snorts and bleats of the western Arctic caribou herd. The pregnant females had left the forest and were migrating by the tens of thousands to their calving grounds on the tundra. The bulls and adolescents would follow later.

As the murmur swelled into a drone, Kapu paced the riverbank. He mapped the course of the herd using his senses—smell, taste, sight, sound, and, through the pads of his feet, touch. He paced faster. The caribou were in the territory of the Mountain Pack. They were crossing creek beds eating willows, star gentians, and butterworts. Then they were trotting through Raw Bones's old territory and approaching the Colville River.

Would the herd go east, as it had for so many years, or come back to the grassy Avalik territory? The beta wolf, Zing, Kapu's faithful brother, trotted behind him waiting to be told what to do.

The sun set. The sky grew blue-purple, and the moon, a feeble glow by day, shone like a lamp.

Kapu tensed. He heard the musical click made by the tendons in the legs of the caribou snapping against bones as they walked—a sound only caribou make. He judged the herd to be in the Colville River valley. The river was deep in some places, shallow in others as it braided its way amid stunted alders and grass to the Arctic Ocean. Kapu waited.

The moon set. In the darkness the river gurgled and boiled. Two miles of caribou were throwing themselves into the deeper waters of the Colville and swimming. Others were splashing across the shallows.

Two hours later the moon came up. Like the Arctic sun, the Arctic moon has its long night or long day. In the deep of winter the moon does not set. The sun, on the other hand, does not rise from late November until late January—the long Arctic night. It does not set from early May until early August— the long Arctic day.

In the pale moonlight of March, Kapu—who, like all wolves, could see in the dark as well as in the day—saw a tide of movement. He stopped pacing. The smell of trodden grass and moss filled his nose—his grass, his moss. The western Arctic herd was on Avalik land.

He lowered his haunches, threw back his head, and howled. His canyon-deep voice climbed an octave and faded. He repeated this song of celebration. Aaka sang a note and slid up the musical scale to harmonize with Kapu. Zing glided up to a note lower than Aaka's. Raw Bones found a note below Aaka's. Silver harmonized with him. They howled a chord of harmonizing notes that rose and fell and rose again. Their music gave the wolverines pause. The Arctic foxes listened. Amy was quiet for the first half of the song; then she began howling low and soared up to take a silver note above Kapu's. The princess of the Avaliks had made her debut.

The song ended abruptly. The caribou thundered up the riverbank and out across the tundra. The Avaliks melted into them, gliding quietly like shadows. The caribou paid them no heed. They were bound for their ancestral calving grounds.

Kapu, with faithful Zing at his shoulder, sped into the mass of caribou and split off a small group. He chased along beside them, watching for an animal to stumble or dash off alone in terror.

The isolated group sensed the wolves and put on speed. All were too swift and healthy for the wolves to catch. Kapu did not mind. The caribou were back. With no pups to keep his pack members at the den, he could lead his pack north to the calving grounds and harvest the weak and sick caribou. The Avaliks would become stronger and stronger, and Kapu would grow in wisdom and experience until he was as grand as his father, and Raw Bones would forever be subdued.

The birth of wolf pups in late May and early June is well timed for both prey and predator. When the female caribou are dropping their calves, the wolves are at their dens raising pups. This gives the calves six weeks or more to grow and develop their running skills. As for the wolves, it is to their advantage not to prey on the calves. A herd could be wiped out by overharvesting the helpless young.

But this year Kapu had changed the biological plan. No pups. He and his wolves would travel right into the midst of the calving grounds and regain their strength and vigor during the summer. They would eat well. Next year, when they were healthy and strong, they would have super pups. Only super wolf pups can survive in the wilderness.

Yet Kapu loved pups. Pups aroused the most

tender emotions in him and all wolves. Those emotions were so strong, they could overflow to pups not their own. When Kapu was young, his parents, Amaroq and Silver, had nurtured a lost girl-pup. She had learned to speak wolf with whimpers and posturing and had endeared herself to them. She had shared Kapu's puppy food and romped with him when he spanked the ground inviting her to play.

As Kapu became friends with the girl-pup, a name for her formed in his mind. It was a scent name: Willow. She smelled of the tiny tundra willows she had crept through to join him and his brothers and sister at their den. She was a puppy herself, and so she became Willow Pup.

Many months later, when she went back to her people, he heard them call her "Julie" and added that sound to his scent, sound, and sight picture of her. She was Willow Pup Julie. The wolf names of the Avaliks were changed by their association with Julie. Kapu's wolf name had been Wind Caller for his lilting voice, Zing's Berry Brother, and Silver's Saxifrage, a scented plant she liked to roll in. But Willow Pup Julie had named them only with sound—Kapu, Zing, and Silver. The sounds were vivid, and they began to know each other by Julie's names for them.

Willow Pup Julie became more than a playmate to Kapu. She was a mother-sister. She had nursed him back to health after a hunter in a roaring metal bird had sent a bullet into his flesh and another had killed his father. Her care had inspired in him a deep loyalty. It was the love he felt for his parent alphas, and the love that dogs, the descendents of wolves, feel for their masters.

After Willow Pup Julie returned to her people pack, devoted Kapu checked on her often. He would stop out of sight of her home and call her back to her pack. She would answer with concern in her howl, and he would go away. She was afraid for him.

In the purple darkness of winter Kapu had found Aaka, the graceful rime-gray daughter of Storm Alarm and Star Gentian, leaders of the Lower Colville River Pack. They lived east of the Avaliks and were a powerful tribe of nine. Amaroq had respected the Lower Colville wolves. He had marked the border between their properties with stronger messages than on any other border.

When Aaka was two years old, she became tired of helping Storm Alarm and Star Gentian with their puppies. She wanted her own. On a sunny afternoon she stole into the no-wolf land between the Avaliks and the Lower Colvilles and hid in the scrubby alders. She listened and waited for Kapu to find her. She had liked him for a long time.

Aaka and her pack had read messages on the wind telling how young Kapu had struggled to hold the Avaliks together. Nails, his father's second in command, had fought Kapu for leadership and lost. Tail between his legs, he had run off, taking with him Kapu's siblings Sister and Zat, who became his beta wolf.

A few weeks later Zit, Kapu's third brother, was killed by a hunter, and the once-magnificent Avalik River Pack dwindled to three: Kapu, Silver, and Zing. The Lower Colvilles began moving into Avalik territory. With Zing as his backup and Silver as the experienced elder, Kapu had held his land against them with howls and scent marking.

So Aaka knew all about Kapu, and Kapu was keenly aware of Aaka. He liked her. Her voice was the only one in the Lower Colville chorus with a little tune to it. Sometimes he would hear her from miles away and wag his tail.

When she slipped into the no-wolf zone, she did not have to wait long for an invitation from Kapu. He saw her enter and gave two soft whimpers, and she romped over the border. The young monarch and his loyal partner, Zing, welcomed her.

Silver did not. She departed almost immediately to make room for the new female leader. She headed for the Upper Colville River Pack, where she knew Raw Bones lived alone and needed a mate. The alpha male and alpha female of a wolf pack are not related. Family members do not mate.

In March of that year Aaka became pregnant. Kapu was young for a wolf father, but leadership had matured him. One evening, at Aaka's urging, he, Zing, and Aaka went off to check the den where Aaka would give birth. They trotted many miles to the old den where Kapu and Zing had been born. Aaka did not like the site and ran off to take charge of the den hunting. After many days she found a steep embankment on the Avalik River. Halfway down was a bench formed by the river. On it grew tiny flowers. She stepped around them and began to dig into the permafrost. The work was slow and difficult, for the earth was frozen hard. Kapu and Zing helped her. After many hours the three wolves jogged off to hunt.

They returned to the site frequently for the next two months and finally managed to chip out a shallow den. The site pleased them all. For miles around poppies and cotton flowers colored the landscape white and yellow. Snow buntings tinkled their songs from grass tufts and moss cushions. Ground-nesting birds—redpolls, longspurs, and horned larks—flitted up from the flowers in explosions of wings. In early June in this delightful environment, Aaka crawled into the whelping den.

Only one pup was born, a little female. Aaka had not eaten well enough for more embryos to develop. All her strength went into making one big, strong pup. She licked and cleaned and loved her pup so much, she became known as Sweet Fur.

But the little family was in trouble. There were no caribou. They hunted ground squirrels and rabbits and even lemmings.

One day in summer, when Sweet Fur was cutting her molars, Willow Pup Julie walked up the river to the white beach near the den. Kapu greeted her cautiously, then with pleasure. Julie got down on all fours. He licked her cheek and released ambrosia around her from the gland on the top of his tail. The sweet scent fell on Julie and again turned her into an Avalik.

Willow Pup Julie camped on the beach. Aaka was afraid of the girl, but eventually came to love her as Kapu did. As a supreme gesture of her trust, she asked Willow Pup Julie to baby-sit Sweet Fur while she ran off to hunt with Kapu and Zing.

The girl called Sweet Fur "Amy," and before long the wolves knew her as Sweet Fur Amy.

After many days had passed, Willow Pup Julie put Sweet Fur Amy into her pack and walked toward the Colville River. Kapu, Aaka, and Zing followed their pup. They were not concerned that the girl would harm Sweet Fur; they simply wanted to be with her.

At the border of their property Kapu stopped. Wolf rules of territory prevented him from taking another step. Beyond lay a strange and dangerous land, the no-wolf zone.

After much indecision Kapu howled a low, wistful note of invitation to his mother, Silver, who was on the other side of the river. He knew she was there. She knew he was there.

Then Willow Pup Julie walked over the Avalik boundary and into the no-wolf zone. When she was not attacked, Kapu whisked his tail as he remembered: Willow Pup Julie was not a wolf but a person, and wolves did not attack people.

Willow Pup Julie, heavily weighted with scent messages, put Sweet Fur Amy on the ground, then crossed the grassy river bottom and splashed into the water. She entered Upper Colville Pack land.

From the embankment Kapu heard her call,

"Silver," her name for his mother. He wagged his tail. Sweet Fur Amy wagged her tail, too, but not for the same reason. Braided among the rich odors of the river, the fish, plants, and ermine, she had picked out a family scent. A wolf over there was her grandmother. She whimpered the grandmother call.

The grandmother answered.

Kapu looked at his daughter. She was pounding her front paws excitedly. He lifted his lips in a smile. The bold move to invite two packs to join forces would work. This wonderful little pup with her keen sense of smell would bond with her grandmother. There would be five loving wolves, as well as the ambitious Raw Bones.

The six made a skilled family of hunters, and they all lived through a harsh and relentless winter.

Now it was spring—a spring to favor the wolves. The caribou were back. With Kapu's good planning they would eat well and grow strong. No pups.

As the caribou moved north, the Avaliks moved north, stopping to feast on caribou that had died of natural causes, or on weak ones that they could isolate and fell. They put on weight. Their fur began to glisten again. They raced north slightly ahead of the great caribou herd, their heads high, their tails straight out behind them. Kapu grew in confidence,

and Raw Bones dropped farther behind the young alpha.

Near the Avalik River, Kapu smelled willow, a very special willow: Willow Pup Julie. With a bound he led his pack around and in front of the browsing caribou and came into Kangik head up, tail up. His pack followed like wind dancers. Their muscles rippled under flowing fur. They ran close together, friendly, loving.

Kapu stopped a distance from Willow Pup Julie. He sought her eyes to tell her he was pleased to see her. She understood and dropped to her knees. But she was afraid for him. She warned him away. Then he saw Kapugen, the hunter. He did not smell his gun or see any aggression in his stride, so he walked toward them.

The musk oxen caught his attention. They were outside the corral where Kapugen kept them to raise and harvest their wool. An amusing wolf thought struck him. Chase them.

Off he went, telling Willow Pup Julie through body language and attitude that this was a wolf joke. She read it and smiled.

The musk oxen, after a brief panic, read the wolf message, too. They did not form a circle with their bony heads out, as they usually did when attacked by wolves. They trotted lightly, spread out, and grazed.

The Avaliks romped in and out among the musk oxen until they had had enough fun and their tongues were hanging out from overheating. Then they ran off a short distance and watched Willow Pup Julie and her father disappear in the frozen mist. With his extraordinary wolf ears Kapu tracked them back to Kangik. Faintly he heard the door of their green house close.

A quick glance at his pack said, "Follow me," and the Avaliks jogged back toward the caribou now thundering into view. Julie's wolves heard their bleating voices and snorting noses, and they saw the antlers of the females ride above the mass of bodies like a forest of dead sticks.

Kapu had not gone far when he was startled by a faint message he had ignored since Raw Bones had led Silver off among the caribou last week.

Silver was pregnant. He stopped running.

Pups.

He was not angry. Pups under any conditions are thrilling. He announced the news with a soft, wavering howl. The pack responded as wolves do to the song of pups. They praised each other by licking chins and cheeks. They chased each other in circles. Then they gathered around Kapu—all but Raw Bones.

He snarled. He had challenged Kapu's leadership by siring puppies, and as the father he was demanding to be recognized as leader.

He snapped at young Kapu. Kapu did not snap back, and because he did not, Raw Bones could not fight. He needed a response in order to do battle. There was none.

Pups. Although these pups threatened his rank and leadership, Kapu ignored their father's challenge. He gathered the dancing pack around him. Pups!

Kapu's love of pups surged through him. He felt no rancor, no jealousy. Pups were coming. Pups were magic. Thin and winter weary as the Avaliks were, they lovingly rubbed against each other, sniffed noses, and licked cheeks. Pups were coming.

When the celebration was over, Raw Bones walked stiff-leggedly toward Kapu to fight. Kapu ignored him again. The young alpha took off. He would lead the pup-happy wolves to the whelping den where Sweet Fur Amy had been born. The flower-bedecked den above the white stony beach was the soul of the Avaliks—the birthing place.

Kapu and his pack flowed like water on the still, flat tundra. Raw Bones closed in behind Kapu. The rangy father-to-be shouldered him, trying to force him toward his ancestral den on the Upper Colville

River. It had been in Raw Bones's family for twenty-five years. Kapu would have none of it. He raised the fur on his neck and back until he appeared twice as big as he was. "I am leader," he was saying, and sprinted on ahead. Zing passed Raw Bones and took his place behind Kapu. Raw Bones dropped into third place.

Aaka ran beside Silver, sharing the affection that the coming of pups creates between females.

Kapu turned into the wind. The pack turned into the wind. Their ruffs and manes swept back. They squinted to protect their eyes until they could barely see where they were going. They did not need to see. They were on the snow-covered trail to their den. Their guides were the sounds of the stunted willows jangling to their right and the sigh of the reindeer moss beneath the wind-packed snow. And there was another guide: their innate sense of direction. They knew at all times exactly where they were.

A long-tailed jaeger flew over the wolves. The bird saw them running hard, which usually meant they were hunting. A wolf kill is a banquet for mammals and birds. The jaeger looked down on the ribbon of wolves and followed them. Then they took to the open tundra and traced graceful S's, not the V-shaped formation of a pack about to make a kill. The bird turned away toward the frozen Arctic Ocean.

The Avalik Pack reached their nursery den on the riverbank. Kapu got down on his side and clawed through the snow to the den entrance. He raked out grass and wind-blown debris.

Silver sniffed the den. It smelled of Aaka and Sweet Fur Amy. She backed away. She was not pleased. She would seek the den where Kapu and Zing had been born.

Raw Bones felt her discontent. "Come with me," he whimpered, and started off for his family den on the Colville River embankment. He loped into the ice mist and was gone. Silver did not follow him.

Kapu let him go.

Silver was not housecleaning but looking off to the north. Sweet Fur Amy sensed her grandmother's reluctance to den clean and scrambled through the entrance. She dug furiously, piling up icy stones. When she backed out, Zing went in. He kicked the stones and dirt out onto the playground as his contribution to the family.

It was the smell of the earth and the sight of everyone working that finally inspired Silver. She crawled into the tunnel and all the way back to the nursery. With her forepaws she dug the room wider, then scooped out a cozy bed for her pups and herself.

She was content with the Avalik den.

Raw Bones returned as Silver came out of the den. The low rumbles of protest in his chest were audible as he entered the group, but he stopped complaining when he looked at Silver. Her face had softened. She wore the gentle look of an expectant wolf mother who had found a place for her pups. She glanced at him. His pups, her eyes said, would be born here. Her digging the nursery had worked the magic.

Good news for the Avaliks. They wagged their tails and exchanged scents. Pups here at the family site.

This decided, Kapu looked north. The pack must now put on the muscle and fat needed to raise tough, energetic wolf puppies. Thanks to Raw Bones they did not have much time.

For the next month and a half they wandered their huge territory searching for the caribou. The female caribou had spread out seeking solitude and isolation to give birth. They were secretive and difficult to find.

One morning near the Colville River, Sweet Fur Amy pricked up her ears and took in short sniffs of air. Then she broke into a sprint.

Kapu followed. She was on the trail of a caribou.

Although he could not smell it himself, he trusted Amy. She could pick up scents five and six miles away and track them down. All wolves have incredible noses lined with hundreds of scent receptors, but Amy was extraordinary for even a wolf. He let her take the lead pointing their way into the wind.

They came upon a female caribou on the open flats. Everyone stopped, listened, looked, and sniffed. Eye messages from Kapu sent the wolves fanning out around the prey. Aaka, whose talent was herding, ran wide to bring the caribou toward the others. The hunters lowered their bodies and stalked slowly forward. The caribou sensed their intent and bolted.

She ran far ahead of the wolves. They slowed their pace, looking this way and that as if not at all interested in hunting. The cow stopped fleeing and browsed. When her head was down, the wolves stole closer. With two glances Kapu directed Silver to the right and Raw Bones to the left. Raw Bones saw an opportunity to cut off the leader and take his place, but he was not fast enough. Kapu saw what he was up to and put on a burst of speed, and he, Zing, and Amy charged the caribou. She lifted her head and ran nimbly away.

Ten times they tried to fell her. Ten times they failed. They gave up the chase. The life of a wolf is hard. Panting, their tongues hanging out of their mouths, they scanned the tundra for prey. The only movements were flowers and grasses dancing in the wind. Raw Bones sneaked up on the young leader and tried to ride up on him. A wolf statement of dominance. Kapu threw him off with a twist.

Suddenly a wolverine not far away startled a caribou to her feet. Infested with parasites, the cow had been resting on a last patch of snow. Her flashing departure set the wolves on a chase.

Within the half hour the hungry pack had their quarry. Raw Bones ran in to eat first as alpha males do. Kapu grabbed the scruff of his neck and pulled him away to let Silver eat first. Raw Bones snarled and grabbed Kapu by the throat, but the young alpha twisted him down. Snarling viciously above him, Kapu held him down on his belly with his regal posture until Silver and then Aaka had eaten. Then he let him up. Raw Bones must be kept in line. He was close to usurping the leadership by virtue of his age and his high rank as the father of Silver's pups. Winning a fight would do it. Kapu kept watch.

When each wolf belly bulged with the good food, Kapu led them to the top of a nearby frost heave, where he rode up on Raw Bones's back to say, "I am alpha." Raw Bones's forehead went perfectly smooth and his eyes became slitlike in submission. He got the message. The others licked Kapu's face and neck, and all tails hung free and loose in contentment. After a brief howl to their alpha, they made wolf beds by scratching out saucers and circling three or four times. Then they lay down and slept like wolves, deeply on one side of their brains, lightly on the other. They slept for almost twenty hours.

On the light side of his sleep Kapu listened to the ravens arriving at the carcass. He heard an Arctic fox yip to his mate to come eat. The low-slung, massive wolverine, who had scared up the prey in the first place, crunched bones in his powerful jaws.

To Kapu food was to be shared. He slept on.

Darkness enclosed the tundra around ten P.M. and lowered the air temperature below zero. A wind drifted the snow over the Avaliks, and they slept and listened—all except Raw Bones. He got up and returned quietly to the kill. Might is right in the wilderness. Knowingly, he ate.

When Raw Bones was sated, he awoke Silver. She opened her yellow wolf eyes that turned the night light into day. Mouthing her nose gently, he told her he was leader. Then he whimpered, "Come with me," and headed toward the den on the Colville.

Kapu heard the dwarf willows tinkle and lifted

his head to see Raw Bones leaving. Shaking snow from his eyebrows and ears, he checked his mother. She was curled so tightly, he knew she was not about to follow him.

Kapu did not call Raw Bones back.

Hardly had the young alpha settled his nose in his tail fur than the willows tinkled again and Raw Bones returned. Kapu sharpened his senses. He had enemies not only around his borders but within. Raw Bones would kill him if he was not alert.

The wolves feasted and slept, feasted and slept, eating five or six pounds a day. In between major meals Raw Bones went back for snacks. He must grow bigger than Kapu.

When only the calcium-rich antlers and a few bones remained, the wolves traveled on, leaving them for the lemmings and snowshoe rabbits. Pregnant caribou would also chew on them for the calcium.

With all his senses alert now, Kapu tuned in on yet another threat to his leadership of the Avaliks. On a wind rode an aggressive scent from the Nuka River Pack. They held the territory to the west and south. Their scent signal was followed by a howl. They had closed in on Avalik territory and were only a night's trot away. Kapu rotated his ears to fine-tune the sounds to the center of his eardrum, where he could hear best. The Nukas were nine strong.

The Avaliks were six.

When the Nukas howled again that night, they were closer. Kapu arose. The guard hairs stood erect on his back. He beat his tail, twisting it toward them like a saber, threw back his head, and howled. His pack howled, sliding up to their harmonizing notes, sliding down, and fading out. Then all was silent.

The Avaliks rubbed necks and chests over the scent glands on the tops of each other's tails and exchanged odors. Their individual aromas were joined into one scent. The mix said "Avalik." The air reeked with this invisible banner as they set off to meet the Nukas. Raw Bones wore the flag grudgingly, but he wore it.

The Nukas were on Avalik property, lying in one of the ravines cut by ages of snowmelt running to the Colville. The Avaliks stopped at the edge of the dip and barked, "Leave or die."

Low Wind and Moon Seeker, the alpha male and female of the Nukas, barked a snippy "no." With that, Kapu and the Avaliks charged into the ravine.

The Nukas fled. Although they outnumbered the Avaliks, the landowner is victor in the wild.

When the Nukas were out of scent and sight, Kapu lifted his leg and sprayed a grass tussock on his border. In the urine was a raging message. It said, "Stay back of this marker or face the fangs of a powerful wolf." He scratched open the ground with his hind feet to back up his scent message. It was an angry visual remark. Then he ran to the top of the highest swell on the flat land and, lifting his head, tail, and ears, calmly and serenely posed. He was saying, "I am the alpha of this land we have scent marked." Even Raw Bones felt his nobility and instinctively lowered his ears and tail in deference. He rumbled his jealousy.

Kapu scent marked again. He was followed by Zing. Although Zing was a male, he did not lift his leg to mark. Only the alpha male and alpha female can do that. He, Raw Bones, Silver, and Sweet Fur Amy must squat.

Raw Bones would not accept his low-ranking status. He lifted his leg in defiance. Kapu went stiff-legged and stared at him. Raw Bones squatted.

Aaka proudly lifted her leg and sprayed warnings to the Nukas.

When the southwestern border was thoroughly drenched, Kapu led his pack north. After a short lope, he turned around and went alone back to his border. He doused it once more. This very area had been a battle zone between the Nukas and the

Avaliks for generations. Amaroq, Kapu's father, had killed the Nuka alpha here, and so had his father before him. Kapu's last message would remind the Nukas of those battles. Scent marking evokes memory and brings peace.

Alert to his territorial duties, Kapu led his pack on a long circular trip scent marking borders. Theirs was a big land. It included much of the caribou calving grounds and Kangik. It stretched from west of the Avalik River south to the banks of the Upper and Lower Colville. On the north it ended far south of Barrow and Wainwright. That territory belonged to Iñupiat Eskimo hunters, a pack to be wary of.

The long legs of the Avaliks carried them as smoothly as shadows. They paced along almost continuously, stopping briefly to look over their herd, mark borders, and gypsy on in the manner of winter wolves.

When possible, Kapu put his scent over the faint but still discernible scent of his father. He let it be known that he, the new leader of the Avaliks, was gaining the power of the departed Amaroq. He must gain all the power and status he could before fatherhood put Raw Bones at the top of the hierarchy.

Raw Bones for his part was plotting the overthrow. At each scent-marking stop he lingered over the messages to learn more about Kapu. He did not like what he read. Kapu was fearless, the essential attribute of a leader. He was also calm, and of good humor and abundant health. But Kapu also revealed in his scent messages that he was young and inexperienced. Raw Bones was old and experienced. He could win.

On one of the trips to houseclean the den, Kapu went into the tunnel to dig and leave his mark on the family home. When he came out, Raw Bones was snarling above him. A wolf alarm rang inside Kapu. He was low, his head beneath Raw Bones's. He was in second position. Surprised at how easily Raw Bones had gained the alpha posture, he lingered as beta almost too long. Another few seconds in this humble stance and Raw Bones would dominate. But Kapu came out of the den with a high leap and landed on Raw Bones's neck snarling savagely. He was backed up by a growling Zing and Aaka. Raw Bones pasted back his ears and slunk away, but he was not done. He would wait until Kapu was alone before attacking again.

That opportunity came soon. One misty dawn the pack bedded down south of Kangik, and Kapu trotted off alone to the rise above Julie's house. Raw Bones watched, then sped down the riverbed out of Kapu's scent range. He waited for him below the rise.

Kapu appeared in the April fog. His fur was shining with silver icelets. He stopped and looked down on the green wooden house. Raw Bones bellied toward him, avoiding dwarf trees that would jangle.

But Kapu was attuned to the tundra. He sensed Raw Bones through his paws and threw himself downhill upon him. Raw Bones got a jaw hold on his shoulder. He pulled Kapu down the slope and twisted him onto his back. Kapu was belly up in the loser's position. This should have been his dethronement, but youth, not experience, counted here. Buckling his young body, Kapu pressed all four paws on Raw Bones's throat and cut off his air. The would-be usurper backed off, and Kapu jumped to his feet. Kapu rode up on Raw Bones before the older wolf could leap. Kapu's head was higher, his chest and his tail were higher, and he growled until Raw Bones lowered himself to the ground. Then he let him up.

Once more Raw Bones had lost. He slunk off, ears pressed back, tail down. Zing came over the rise. Raw Bones rushed him, but youthful Zing stared at him and displayed his white fangs. "I am the beta," he said.

Raw Bones disappeared in the early-morning ice mist.

Kapu turned his attention to the green house now

taking form as the air warmed and cleared. There near the river Peter Sugluk, the young hunter-dancer, and Willow Pup Julie were hitching the dogs to the sled. Kapu sensed their pleasure in each other's company. Peter was Julie's alpha male. He wagged his tail and howled to them, "Come home to us."

Willow Pup Julie snapped a dog into his traces and straightened up. She looked in his direction and called gently, "Someday, someday." Kapu howled again. This time he drew his tongue up and down in his pursed mouth, undulating his tone. Julie harmonized with him. Then they abruptly stopped and spoke no more.

Listening to the mysterious wild language, Peter said, "It would be good to live close to the wolves and nature as our elders did. There is much to learn about ourselves out there."

"Ee-lie," answered Willow Pup Julie, and called once more to Kapu. He did not answer. He was busy. The scent of an arthritic caribou had drenched the wind, and he had gone off to locate it.

Raw Bones returned to the pack in its camp south of Kangik and nosed Silver awake. He would take her back to his old territory, where he was king. She growled. She did not want to go. He lay down and his back fur bristled.

The border check went on for weeks. The more Kapu scent marked his territory, the stronger he felt and the more peaceful the pack became. Slowly Kapu was healing the devastating loss of the great Avalik alpha male wolf Amaroq. Social harmony was being restored as Kapu developed leadership skills. When he was truly in charge, Raw Bones would not be able to challenge him.

That glorious moment was not yet in sight. Raw Bones's disposition worsened. Unable to dethrone Kapu, he began to nip at Sweet Fur Amy. Her keen sense of smell had raised her to a rank above him. She had become a second beta, equal to Zing. As father of the pups-to-be Raw Bones deeply resented this. If he could not be alpha, he must certainly be beta. At every opportunity he bared his teeth and wrinkled his forehead to threaten her into battle. But Sweet Fur Amy would not fight back, and this rendered Raw Bones annoyingly helpless.

Sweet Fur Amy's talent developed. She learned to recognize sick animals not only by scent but by subtle limps, the tilt of a head, and the droop of eyes. She no longer wasted the pack's time on the healthy. When she picked out a feeble animal, she signaled the news to Kapu and he let her take the lead, much to Raw Bones's displeasure.

In daylight and shadow, whenever the opportunity arose, the resentful Raw Bones gave Sweet Fur Amy a painful smack with his rear end. She controlled her desire to fight. He was bigger and older. She could not possibly win.

But she did not like it. When the pack was resting, she strengthened her neck muscles by thrashing heavy caribou hides from side to side. She strengthened her leg muscles chasing the fleet-footed Zing. She ate often. Her black fur reflected blue lights, and her body grew hard and muscular. Raw Bones with all his nastiness was forcing her to become a more powerful wolf than he.

The sun stayed up longer and longer. From twelve hours above and twelve hours below the horizon at the March equinox, it was up all but a few hours in late April. During this time Sweet Fur Amy's ability to find weak and sick animals dramatically increased the Avaliks' hunting success. It rose from one try in ten to one in five. With abundant food they put on muscle and weight.

In the second week of May the sun stayed up night and day. Without trickle or sound most of the tundra snow vanished in vapor. The birds returned to their grassy nesting grounds by the tens of thousands. The Avaliks ran in constant sunlight. They split caribou herds into smaller groups by running through them. They checked each individual, noted the pregnant females and those with calves. They noted the healthy and pinpointed the sick and old for harvesting at some later date.

One foggy hour in early June, Silver spoke to her son, Kapu, with her eyes. "Pups." With a right about-face he led the pack to the den on the Avalik River embankment. The alpha male wolf leads the pack to the den when the mother-to-be gives the signal. Raw Bones snarled as he followed Kapu and Silver. The young alpha had taken over this ceremony that would have elevated him to that rank.

The next day the pups were born. The wolves wandered out on the tundra away from the den. They whined, flashed their tails, and howled in celebration. Far to the west the Nukas heard and pricked up their ears and hurried out to mark their eastern border. More Avaliks had been born.

Ten days after the birth of the pups, Silver came out of the den. Tails wagged, feet pranced, tongues licked cheeks and faces. Now pack members would know how many pups had been born. Kapu let Raw Bones listen first; then he and Aaka listened. Sweet Fur Amy and Zing listened. Each wolf cocked its ears until the tiny voices were counted: two—that was all.

The famine had taken its toll on Silver's body, but the vigorous swishing of tails spoke of the pack's pride.

Two or ten, it mattered not. The Avaliks had pups. Kapu dashed to the top of the embankment, sat down, lifted his head, and sang. He was joined by all but Silver, who had gone back into the den. The others whimpered, squeaked intimately and softly to each other, then howled as if a big litter of fat puppies had been born. The pup serenade done, Kapu, Sweet Fur Amy, and Zing sped off to hunt for food for the mother. Raw Bones ran last until he saw that Sweet Fur Amy was only a few paces in front of him. He bolted past her.

They had not gone far before Kapu stopped. He lifted his head and tasted the wind coming off the Avalik River. With a glance at his pack to say, "Stay where you are," he ran back toward the river. Raw Bones took this opportunity to strike Sweet Fur Amy with another hard whack. Again she did not react. She cricked her tail to express her annoyance, but she would not fight.

Serenely she opened her nostrils and breathed in the scent image of Willow Pup Julie. She was not far away. Kapu had gone back to greet her. Sweet Fur Amy sat down. Zing and Raw Bones sat down.

Willow Pup Julie was sitting on the white stone beach where she had met Kapu last summer. She was calling the ground squirrels out of their burrows with the little whistle she wore around her neck. She was dressed in a flowered summer parka and blue jeans. Her thick black hair fell to her shoulders. Her beautiful face was serene. Kapu whimpered. She looked up.

"Ee-lie, Kapu." She got to her knees. She did not move, giving Kapu time to adjust to her. Presently he spanked the ground in wolf pleasure and greeted her with the family whimper of affection. She whimpered back and he ran toward her, whisking his tail.

"I came to see the pups," she said, looking eagerly toward the den.

Kapu did not understand her words, but he understood why she had come. Much wolf talk goes on through the eyes, and Willow Pup was looking at the nursery.

"You have puppies, all right," she said. "But they are still young. They're not out of the den. I don't see them. I'll come back another day." But instead of leaving, she sat down.

She patted the stones at her side. "May I see them?" she asked. He stood perfectly still. "Come here," she said. Kapu did not accept the invitation, nor did he look into her eyes.

"Ee-lie," she laughed. "You are a leader, all right. No one can tell you what to do." Kapu looked away, then back, and walked closer.

"You are lean," she said, noting how the black fur parted over his shoulders and clung to his ribs. "You are hunting long hours. The pups and their mother need lots of food, all right."

Kapu dropped to his belly. Slowly he turned his head and stared at her. His large yellow eyes with their black pupils pulled her unblinkingly into his world. She willingly came along and was part of his family again.

With that Willow Pup Julie began to talk.

"Kapu," she said, "my little brother, Amaroq, your father's namesake, is running. He's not quite a year old. That's very unusual. He must have your spirit in him."

She went on. "The boy-pup keeps me busy chasing him. He runs to the umiaq. I try to catch him. He runs to the river. I try to catch him. He is very fast." Kapu did not understand these messages, but he did understand other scents that she carried on her person. She was living with her father and stepmother and someone else, a baby. Peter Sugluk had not been around lately.

After Willow Pup Julie stopped speaking, she

and Kapu sat in silence, enjoying each other's company. They watched the fish swim upstream and the redpolls sing from tiny three-inch-high willows. Their eyes followed a snowy owl swooping down on a lemming and watched two ravens eating birds' eggs.

The sun dipped to the horizon, hung there for a while, then started up the sky again. Kapu and Willow Pup Julie arose simultaneously. As if they had talked it over, each went home. Julie walked down the river shore; Kapu climbed the embankment.

He found Silver stretched out in the vermilion sunlight, taking a rest from the puppies. Raw Bones was on his belly looking into the den. He tilted his head from side to side, picking up subtle odors that informed him one pup was a male and one was a female. Raw Bones wagged his tail once and withdrew. Aaka listened.

The pups' whimpers were weak. Aaka wrinkled her brow and let Sweet Fur Amy take her turn. She too was disturbed by the weak whimpers. Slowly she pulled back, but before she could get to her feet, Raw Bones jumped on her.

Amy reared and hit him with her back, then vaulted away. Raw Bones stalked her, snarling for a fight. Again Sweet Fur Amy refused. This sweet-tempered wolf was growing very tired of Raw Bones's heckling her. When he growled again, she suddenly knew what to do. Lifting her head, she sniffed the air. Her ears went up and her eyes sharpened with excitement to say, "I smell a very sick caribou." The pack arose. Sweet Fur Amy glanced at Kapu and sent him a different message.

He answered by starting the hunt. The Avaliks followed. No sooner were they on their way than Kapu fell back with Aaka and Zing, and Sweet Fur Amy took the lead.

Raw Bones put on speed, passed Zing and Kapu, snarled past Aaka, and took second position. No wolf objected. Aaka, the herder, moved to her position at the side of the pack and loped along gracefully. Occasionally she stopped to investigate the bearberry plants now sweet with tiny flowers.

The tundra rolled out in all directions, spreading wide and gold-green. The wind blew gently. The warm sun coaxed cushions of starwort flowers into bloom.

The Avaliks ran several miles before Raw Bones caught the scent of Sweet Fur Amy's prey. When he was certain he had the trail, he knocked her out of first place and took the lead. She did not object.

Holding a steady pace Raw Bones led the Avaliks down the river valley, up onto the tundra, and into a ravine carved by snowmelt. He was leader of the pack. He thrust his head high. He lifted his tail into alpha position. The pack came on. Running full out, he came upon a huge bull caribou. His new antlers of the year were dark with velvet.

Raw Bones gave orders to the pack and rushed him. The bull did not run. He reared. His cleaver-sharp hoofs slashed toward Raw Bones and hit the ground with the power of a falling meteor, missing their mark by inches. The bull reared to strike again.

Raw Bones drew back. Sick animals do not charge. He signaled Aaka to close in. She was nowhere around. He glanced behind him. The pack sat in a wide semicircle looking at him. The bull saw them, turned, and jogged off. His tendons snapped like bongo drums. Snowmelt splashed up from his footsteps.

Raw Bones dashed after him. With little effort the bull left him far behind. He disappeared in the dim light of the midnight sun.

Raw Bones slowed and stopped, tongue hanging out from overheating. Feeling peculiar, he glanced back at his pack. They were looking at him and smiling at Sweet Fur Amy's wolf joke. He growled for a full five minutes.

On the way home Sweet Fur scented an old cow

with torturous botfly infestations. She glanced at Kapu. Her eyes said, "This is no joke"—and they were off. Within two hours the pack had eaten well. Kapu encouraged Raw Bones to carry a hindquarter back to Silver.

And the wholeness of the pack was restored.

In June the sun rose to its highest point in the Arctic sky. Life responded. The tundra flittered with young mammals and fledgling birds learning to pounce, fly, and play—all but the Avalik pups. Tiny Whimper and No Growl—this was how the wolves now thought of them—did not leave the den. They were long overdue to come out and romp on the playground.

Something was wrong. Silver went into the nursery and picked up Tiny Whimper by the scruff of the neck. She carried her outside and gently put her down. The little pup could not walk. Her baby-blue eyes looked from Kapu to Silver. She whimpered a thin squeak. Silver went back for No Growl and placed him beside his sister.

The Avaliks paced anxiously around the pups, nosing and licking them. They cricked their tails in uncertainty and puzzled over them. Then they lay down and put their heads on their paws. The pups were doomed to death. Silver had not recovered from the winters of famine. She could not give them enough milk.

Kapu watched in distress. The pups were in trouble. He blinked and cocked his head to one side and then the other.

Aaka lay down beside them. She licked Tiny Whimper first and then No Growl, trying to get their blood flowing and to stimulate them to walk. They were too weak.

Kapu suddenly pricked up his ears and looked toward the Avalik River. With a swing of his tail he bounded down the embankment and trotted along the shore to meet Willow Pup Julie.

"Kapu," she called. "Kapu, I'm back." He knew why she had come. He did not take time to adjust to her presence but let her scramble up the embankment to the playground.

"Ee-lie." She dropped to her knees. "The little pups are sick."

She picked up listless Tiny Whimper. Silver and Aaka watched intently. Willow Pup Julie whimpered wolf pup talk and stroked the little head. She held one limp paw between her fingers.

"Kapu," she said, "I must take the pups home, all right. I will feed them rich milk from bottles. When they are strong, I will return them to you." Kapu stared into her eyes. He understood her intent by the mothering tone in her voice. He did not take the pup back, nor did Silver come for them. Julie tucked fragile Tiny Whimper into her parka and glanced at Aaka and Sweet Fur Amy to see if they objected. They did not reach for the puppy. Their alpha had not, so they would not. Kapu was beginning to direct the behavior of the pack. The pups would go with Willow Pup Julie. Although they responded to Kapu's wish, each individual quickly expressed its feelings. Aaka walked to Kapu's side and nuzzled his chin. Sweet Fur Amy took a deep breath of Julie in through her nostrils and relaxed her tail and face. The pups were in loving hands. Silver lay wearily on her side, and Raw Bones slunk off to the top of the embankment, put his head on his paws, and rumbled a protest from deep in his chest. Zing, the loyal beta, kept his eye on the disgruntled Raw Bones, whose rank was about to sink to an all-time low without the pups.

Kapu was close to achieving the highest form of wolf government—leadership that holds strong individuals together but allows for personalities and feelings. Kapu was close to greatness. He lifted his head high.

Feeling the pack was with her, Willow Pup Julie

put No Growl into her parka with Tiny Whimper and pressed them close to her body.

"They'll be all right," she said, locking her gaze on Silver's golden eyes. The mother looked away. After a moment she turned and looked unblinkingly into Julie's eyes. "Trust" was the message. With a soft whimper of affection, Willow Pup Julie walked down the embankment to the river's edge and strode off along it. Released from ice by the sun, the water chortled and leaped beside her, accompanying her happy song—"Pups, little pups, little pups."

When she was out of scent range, the Avaliks milled in a small knot, passing scent, passing mood, passing love, reaching a decision. Then they trod lightly down the embankment. They walked behind Willow Pup Julie and their pups until they came to their favorite resting site on the outskirts of Kangik. There they listened quietly as their Willow Pup opened the door of the green house and went inside. Gusts from within smelled of Kapugen; his wife, Ellen; and their son, Amaroq. The wolves inhaled deeply, sat down on their haunches, and waited for their pups to come out.

Julie's wolves stayed on the knoll for many sleeps. When it became apparent that the pups were not going to come out, Kapu went down the path and tasted the air that surrounded the house with tongue and nose. There was no scent of Tiny Whimper or No Growl, just the odors of rich milk, the sweet scent of a human baby, and people. He returned to the pack, whimpered a message, then threw back his head and howled in misery. The Avaliks sang a song of the lost and missing.

When their chorus had diminished down the scale and into silence, Raw Bones and Silver curled up to sleep. Zing, Kapu, and Aaka jogged off to hunt in the orange light of the ever-circling summer sun that was now climbing toward three o'clock in the morning.

Sweet Fur Amy had her own mission. She walked closer to Julie's home. She had smelled the pups in the heavy mix of scents that surrounded the house. She was kin and baby-sitter to these pups. She could not leave.

PART II

ICE BLINK, THE STRANGER

*F*our hundred miles away a rangy white wolf ran desperately across the border of her territory in the Canadian Arctic. Her eyes were mustard yellow, her muzzle long and regally sharp. She took a bearing on the sun that did not set and, sensing the magnetic forces of the Earth, jogged west into Alaska. A chilling fear had driven her from her beloved home.

The white wolf came to the foothills of the Philip Smith Mountains, where icy snow lingered in the higher elevations. As she crossed a swatch of ice, the sunlight was reflected up onto her white belly for the length of an eye blink.

Sedge Ears, the male leader of the Smith Mountain Pack, saw the flash, and the white wolf became Ice Blink. He watched the stranger.

Ice Blink was in the no-wolf zone that ran along his border. She zigged and zagged, nose to the ground. A scent in a clump of spike moss told her a ptarmigan had been there. A sniff down an Arctic fox den flashed an image of pups. From rock to moss to animal trails she went. Finally she came upon the scented border of the Smith Mountain wolves. She sniffed the information in their urine. The pack consisted of four healthy adults: the alpha male, Sedge Ears; the alpha female, Alder Whisper; the second in command, a wolf with a nameless odor; and a yearling baby-sitter. Her faint scent told Ice Blink she had not been out border marking recently. She must be with the new pups of the year. Pups there were. Alder Whisper's scent was rich with milk.

Ice Blink scent read deeper into the layers of messages. Sedge Ears feared the humans in the valley. Alder Whisper had a stomachache. She had eaten grass to cure it. Over the normal wolf odorous chitchat rose a stronger message—the Smith Mountain Pack had recently killed a strange wolf in their territory.

Ice Blink adjusted her route to avoid them. Keeping their scent on her left and the distant odor of the Shublik Mountain Pack on her right, she continued northwest in the no-wolf zone.

Curious about her, Sedge Ears shook moss bits from his fur and climbed a fungus-freckled slope. The Smith Mountain Pack lived among the caribou bulls that hung out together at this time of year.

They were powerful animals and difficult to fell. Sedge Ears's pack could use another adult, but only a strong and perfect one. He rolled in caribou droppings to disguise himself and stole to the edge of the no-wolf zone. For almost an hour he walked parallel to Ice Blink. Her footfall told him she was a large wolf, well fed, and four years old—in her prime. He liked that, but other things about her made him wary. She was too old to be seeking a new pack and too young to retire alone, as old wolves do. Her scent disturbed him, and he sniffed her air again and again. She bore a strange odor, sickly sweet. It warned him not to invite her into his pack.

Ice Blink knew she had been turned down. She took to a river valley and jogged along shores that frequently smelled of oil. Airplanes had landed in these places and set men free to hunt wolves, moose, and caribou. She knew about airplanes and men. Hastily she trotted out of the river valley and up Salisbury Mountain. The winds blew with such force here that only lichen gardens could live. In this frozen desert water was scant. The ice and snow rarely melted. To survive, the lichens would dry up and wait years for the sun to melt a few drops of water. Then almost instantly they would become a lovely green-gray and grow ever so slightly. The gardens were thousands of years old.

On a slope of these plants, Ice Blink tasted the air for the caribou that savored them. She had just caught the faint scent of several bulls browsing uphill and started after them when a Cessna 185 airplane droned out of the clouds. It circled above her. Ice Blink pulled her tail between her legs and dropped to her belly. Her white fur blended with an ice field. The plane circled three times and then flew off. Ice Blink licked her paw and wiped it over her ears to relieve her nervousness.

The airplane had brought back feelings of distress. Her pack had met with a great misfortune she connected with them. Last autumn such a plane had come out of the sky and landed not far from her pack. A human had stolen to a knoll and shot at her with a dart gun. He had missed, but the gun blast and the man were imprinted on her mind by fear.

About a week later her adolescent sons behaved strangely. They snarled and chased her. Their mouths drooped open, their tongues swelled and drooled saliva. They were hot with fever. She bolted into the dwarf trees to watch them in safety. One son stumbled, fell, and lay still. Almost immediately the other fell. When, after a long time, they did not move, her mother love brought her hesitatingly to their sides.

The alpha son was unable to move. His eyes were open and staring. She smelled his noxious breath and whimpered to him. He did not get up. She turned to her other son and called to him. When he did not respond, she withdrew to the edge of the dwarf trees.

Ice Blink watched as foaming saliva bubbled out of their mouths. She saw them pant heavily. First one and then the other panted no more. They were dead.

Safe in the trees, Ice Blink put her head on her paws and stared into space. Nine members of her pack of eleven had died this way. Only she and her mate, Bear Scratcher, were alive. Her wolf mind flicked quickly from death to life. She needed to be with her breathing, lively mate. Getting to her feet, she sought out Bear Scratcher on a favorite bluff above the river. She lay down beside him. The next morning another plane landed, and an Eskimo and a white man stole toward them. Again they shot darts from guns, and again they missed. Ice Blink and her mate sped away.

"We've got to inoculate them before they spread the rabies to dogs and people," said the Inuttut Eskimo Qignak.

"We'll never do it now," the white man said. "We scared them good." He paused, then added, "Maybe the epidemic won't be too bad. The scientists say very few wolves die of rabies. They're much more likely to die of mange."

"I know these wolves," said Qignak. "They have been dying of rabies—first one, then two, then eight. My family hunts this river valley."

"I understand that," said the white man, "and we're trying to inoculate them, but we may have to give up." He put another tranquilizing dart into his gun and scanned the dwarf trees that grew in the river bottomland. There was not a wolf to be seen.

"The wolves are our brothers," Qignak said in his deep, soft voice.

After the sun rose in January, and before the March breeding season of the wolves, Bear Scratcher awoke beside Ice Blink and moaned in pain. He was hot and feverish. Saliva dripped from his open mouth.

Two days later he attacked her. Terrified, she sped into the no-wolf zone. He would not dare enter the forbidden land.

But he did. Snarling and drooling, her disease-maddened mate bore down on her. Then he, too, fell and lay stiff, unable to move.

Ice Blink crept toward her lifelong companion. He growled through bubbling foam. She came nearer. She licked his saliva-wet cheek, and with that the virus entered her bloodstream through a small wound in her mouth.

Bear Scratcher bit the air, and the stench of the rabies virus filled her nostrils. It smelled of the death that had taken her sons and all the other members of her pack. Ice Blink drew her tail between her legs and crept away.

She came back once. He was dead. Whining softly to herself, she returned to the no-wolf zone and began walking. She would find a new pack far from the disease that had been passed from one family member to another in bites and saliva. Some had died a few days after being bitten; others had carried the virus a month before falling ill. Her mate had carried it for a year.

When the Cessna 185 was out of hearing, Ice Blink trotted across a wind-blasted territory where no wolves lived. She ran steadily like a leaf on a rushing stream.

She covered three hundred miles before she stopped. Ice Blink was in the no-wolf zone that bordered the Lower Colville River Pack, Aaka's original family. Odors in the urine revealed that the pack had no beta. They could use her. She was an experienced adult. Ice Blink hid in the dense grasses that grew in the river valley and waited for an invitation to join them.

Storm Alarm and Star Gentian were aware of her almost as soon as she entered the valley. They scented, listened, and peered through the ground brush at her. Like Sedge Ears, they learned she was capable and that she was looking for a new family. They had room for her, but like Sedge Ears they were wary of her scent messages. Storm Alarm watched her through the leafy bushes, one bright discerning eye sizing her up. Presently the eye vanished. Storm Alarm and Star Gentian walked deeper into their territory.

Ice Blink saw the eye shine in the bushes and snap off. There was no invitation. She lifted her head and ruff and trotted on.

Keeping to the no-wolf zone, the white wolf circled the northern border of the Lower Colville Pack's territory and arrived at the border of the Avalik Pack. They had not been in this part of their territory since pup time and would not be until the pups could run with the pack. That time was not far away. The August sun was setting for an hour or so to mark the night.

Boldly she walked onto their land, exploring every scent and sound, watching every twisting grass blade and fluttering bird. A mile inland she slipped into a forest of two-foot-high aspen trees growing in a drainage and came upon the body of a wolf. It was frozen in packed snow at the bottom of the ravine. Ice Blink could not know that this wolf had been named Nails by Julie. But she did know by the shape of his wounds that he had been killed by a knifelike moose hoof. Ice Blink sniffed for more information. The faded odor of the Avalik Pack was on the mosses around him. They had come to investigate the fallen wolf. She rubbed herself in the Avalik scent and trotted on.

Coming around a frost heave, she saw ravens circling above the horizon, marking a kill.

She broke into a smooth low run and came upon a dead young musk ox. Holes and rips in the carcass were drenched with grizzly bear scent. Ice Blink tasted the air. The bear was not far away, eating blueberries and guarding her kill.

Ice Blink was not concerned about the closeness of this powerful female of the tundra. Wolves and bears often share food. Furthermore, Ice Blink could easily outrun her. She could even turn around in the middle of a sprint and chase the bear.

Ice Blink scared off the ravens and three Arctic foxes, then set upon the food. She was eating with great satisfaction when the bear returned and charged.

The white wolf glided away, her shoulder fur pulsing softly as she ran. Miles along, she settled down in a garden of tundra grass and fell asleep. She was deep in Avalik country.

On the western side of Avalik territory Sweet Fur Amy was leading the pack toward Kangik on the trail of something the others could not yet smell. Knowing her gifts, they simply jogged trustingly behind her, their noses, eyes, and ears scanning the flat, gold-green landscape for game. They saw only a darkening sky.

Sweet Fur Amy came to a halt below the knoll where she often stood to view the green house. Silver, who was far behind, was glad for the rest. She had not recovered her vigor since the pups had been born. Curling up with her head on her tail, she snuggled her nose into her warm fur and shivered. Aaka saw her tremble and lay close beside her to share her own warmth. Kapu watched Silver with concern. Raw Bones ignored her. He was watching Sweet Fur Amy, who on the far knoll was sniffing the prey he ought to be smelling. The threads of air coming to him carried no odor but the cold of an icy wind. Remembering her wolf jokes, he eventually lay down.

Kapu did not. He saw the alertness in Sweet Fur Amy's pose and, nosing Silver gently, walked off to join his daughter. Zing followed him. The two males breathed in deeply but did not smell anything unusual. They glanced at Sweet Fur Amy. Her focused posture was saying, "Put all your senses to work. Excitement is here." Kapu and Zing twisted their ears and expanded their nostrils, but nothing was revealed to them.

The three wolves waited in silence. Behind them the late-August sun turned red-orange. Just before the sun disappeared, the atmosphere flattened it into an oval, and in a blink it was gone. Four hours later it arose. The wolves were still watching the village of Kangik. The wind parted their shiny ruffs as if it were a comb.

Suddenly Kapu and Zing scented the news that Amy already knew. Their pups had not died. They were in the house with Willow Pup Julie.

Kapu whimpered a high, thin call to his pack, a call so high it was out of the range of all ears but theirs. The Avaliks got to their feet and stole softly to the ridge in time to see Kapugen walk out of the house. With him was a fat wolf pup.

"Come, Nutik," Kapugen said to No Growl, who was no longer dying but was a big healthy pup with a new name. "Nutik" means jumper in Iñupiaq. He ran to the man and was rewarded with a fish treat and a hug. "Good, Nutik, good, good."

Kapugen placed him between his legs and slipped a harness over his head and chest, then hitched him to a cart with wheels. Nutik jumped up and down in excitement. Then Willow Pup Julie appeared, carrying Tiny Whimper under one arm.

"Ho, Uqaq, little talking girl," Julie said putting her down.

"WoooOOO, OOOOooo," Tiny Whimper replied, justifying her Iñupiaq name, Uqaq, "to talk." The boy Amaroq and his mother came out of the house and joined the Green House Pack, which consisted of an alpha male and female, Kapugen and Ellen; a beta, Julie; and three pups, Amaroq, Nutik, and Uqaq. They milled and vocalized in the blue light.

Julie picked up her half-brother, Amaroq, and put him in the cart. Uqaq ran in circles. "WoooOOO. WOOOooooo, oooo." She had been named well. The Avaliks patiently waited for the opportunity to walk down the embankment and take back their pups.

"Hut," Kapugen called to Nutik, and he lunged joyfully forward, pressing his big feet to the earth and heading toward the village. Kapugen, Willow Pup, and Uqaq ran beside them. The little boy's mother did not. She smiled, waved, and walked to the school, where she taught in the winter.

Uqaq kept close to Julie's heels. Her need to run in a pack was developing. She kept a small space between herself and Willow Pup's boots, just as she would have done with pups on the tundra.

"Gee," Kapugen shouted to Nutik, who obediently pulled the cart to the right. They went up the rise to the Quonset hut that housed the airplane Kapugen owned and operated. His sled dogs were tied to their kennels at the back of the big structure. They barked at Nutik, then suddenly stopped, sniffed, and burst into a volley of wild barks. The scent of the Avalik pack had reached their noses.

"Wolf, wolf, wolf," they exclaimed furiously.

Kapu heard them tell of their whereabouts and led his pack into the shelter of a thin cloud of mist. He did not wait to see if Kapugen, the hunter, knew what his dogs had said. He ran until he was on the other side of the low cloud. He would wait here until he could get the pups. The pack gathered around him, licking his face and chin excitedly to say the pups were alive and fat.

The days grew dramatically shorter, telling Kapu it was time for the wolves to wander afar. Nevertheless he and his pack stayed near Kangik, keeping out of sight of the town and the dogs. The Avaliks were ready to rescue the pups at the first opportunity.

One morning a large flock of male eider ducks flew in from the nesting grounds along the Arctic coast. By the hundreds they landed on the inland ponds. Hiding in the sedges, they shed all their wing feathers and were unable to fly. In silence they sneaked around the dwarf reeds and water crowfoot waiting for their flight feathers to grow back in.

Kapu watched them arrive with detachment. But when they flew south, lifting off the water by twos, sixes, and hundreds, it was time to change wolf activities. The inner clocks of the caribou were sending them south.

Kapu glanced in the direction of the Brooks Mountain Range. He must lead the Avaliks toward the forests where the caribou wintered. He looked at Aaka. Her rime-gray fur gleamed. She was well fed and strong. She was ready for the rigors of the long, bitter winter of the Arctic. Zing, Raw Bones, and Sweet Fur Amy were also well honed for Arctic wolf life. Silver was not.

This was a problem. A pack is the sum of all its individuals. Kapu would have to slow the pack to Silver's pace.

He was torn. To accomodate his mother, Silver, he must leave now for the forest. On the other hand, the health of the pack depended on waiting for the vigorous pups in the green house in Kangik.

He needed to go. He needed to stay.

Indecision in an alpha male wolf is weakness. Raw Bones saw his chance. But his eyes flickered, telling Kapu he was about to attack. Kapu leaped up and dropped his entire weight on Raw Bones. Raw Bones went down. Kapu snarled, teeth shining in his blue-black face. He held the usurper down by standing stiff-legged across his prone body. Raw Bones shivered.

Kapu opened his mouth wide and barked his annoyance in a deep, guttural voice. He was saying it was taking too much energy to keep Raw Bones in line. He would find a way to end this constant conflict. Snarling viciously above him for almost a minute, he asserted his dominance. The only obstacle to Kapu's becoming as magnificent a leader as his father was this ill-tempered male. And yet he could not kill him. He was his mother's mate. He was a member of the pack.

Suddenly above his threat barks he heard a wolf chorus. He cocked his ears. It was led by Low Wind, the Nuka male leader. He and his pack were on Avalik land. Low Wind had taken advantage of Kapu's plight—a sick mother and pups that held him near Kangik. He had moved into Kapu's territory.

Kapu snarled authoritatively and let Raw Bones up. He swished his tail in the direction of the enemy, and the Avaliks were off to meet the Nukas.

Silver did not join them. She curled into a tight ball and dug her nose into the fur of her tail. Kapu noted her absence and set a swifter pace.

The Avaliks and Nukas met where Avalik borders faded away at a National Petroleum Reserve outpost. The activities of humans had wiped out the wolf borders. Oil and machinery held this territory within the Avalik home range.

They came toward each other with fur rising on their bodies, making them enormous warriors. Kapu eyed Low Wind. Low Wind eyed Kapu. Kapu scratched his signature on the ground with hard strokes of his claws. Low Wind placed his signature on an oily piece of ground, where it could be plainly seen and dreaded. Kapu lifted his leg and scent marked the top of a tundra grass blade. "Come no farther," he said.

Now that Kapu's attention was totally focused on Low Wind, Raw Bones saw his opportunity. With a quick movement he knocked Kapu toward the enemy. Startled, Low Wind attacked Kapu, and so did Raw Bones. Instantly, loyal Zing was upon Raw Bones. Head and chest above him, he bossed him to the ground and pinned him there. Zing had had enough of this wolf too.

The alpha fight began. Kapu and Low Wind mouthed each other's shoulders and rose on hind feet, each trying to lift his head higher than the other's. The growling and snarling was terrifying. Both wolf packs watched in silence. In the midst of the fight Sweet Fur Amy signaled Aaka, and the two sped into the middle of the Nukas. They encircled two adolescents and herded them behind the Avalik lines.

Low Wind, momentarily distracted by the departure of his young adults, turned his head, and in that second Kapu rolled him to the ground. The battle was over. Kapu let Low Wind get back to his feet; then he scratched the ground. Stiff-legged, he walked to a battered oil barrel and shot his scent higher than ever before. Low Wind responded to this statement of victory by pressing his ears against his head and lowering his tail. His face was smooth and expressionless. Kapu's eyes were wide, his tail high, his fur and ears erect. He was magnificent to see. The two leaders looked at each other; then Low Wind signaled his adolescents to return and walked away.

The young Nukas did not move. Kapu, the victor, had told them to stay. Low Wind stepped forward to get them. Kapu lifted the fur on his back and, scratching the ground, drew a new border. He gave Low Wind the oily territory he was on, then turned and walked off with the two strong Nukas. With them in the pack Raw Bones would not be needed.

The rival packs trotted apart. Not far from the battleground Kapu whimpered his joy, sat down, and threw back his head. He howled. His pack howled. The Nukas howled. The wolf music continued until each individual in each pack felt that the business of the day had been concluded satisfactorily.

Then, rising from his haunches, Kapu took time to look at the young Nukas. Storm Call was a male Sweet Fur Amy's age. His back and head were gray as old sea ice, and his dense ruff was tinged with a reddish hue. The other adolescent—his sister, Lichen—was darker and more slender and agile. When Kapu turned his attention to her, she walked right up and licked his cheek to tell him he was her leader and a very good one. Kapu looked from Storm Call to Lichen and invited them into the Avalik Pack. They mixed scents and, pleased with their new family, jogged in silence, following Kapu back to the wolf pups at Kangik.

Along the way Amy picked up the scent of a young caribou and invited Storm Call and the swift-footed Zing to join her. Storm Call hesitated, but when he got Kapu's approval, the three ran wide around the animal. They chased it back to Kapu, Aaka, Raw Bones, and Lichen. It was felled with ceremony and pride. The two new Avaliks were good teammates.

Several hours later, when the wolves were sleeping off their feast, Aaka arose, selected a tasty slice of meat for Silver, and carried it toward Kangik. Wolves care for their weak and unfortunate.

To the north a lone raven flying over the tundra circled Ice Blink. She had come to a road. Snow machines in winter and four-wheel drives in summer had laid it down. Their runners and wheels had broken the plant skin of the tundra, and the sun had poured in and melted the permafrost beneath. The road was now two long lakes of water that would freeze in winter, thaw again, and grow bigger. Human scent all along the road made it a no-wolf zone that needed no scent marking. Wise wolves stayed away.

Ice Blink zigzagged back and forth across it, ignoring the humans and seeking wolf messages. She found none. Her fur swinging, her big white feet lifting and falling rhythmically, she trotted down the road deeper into Avalik country.

Eventually the watery path brought her to the headwaters of the Meade River. Finding no fresh sign of wolf, Ice Blink went on.

On the bank of the Avalik River she picked up a whiff of wolf ambrosia—the perfume of the pack that had visited the dead wolf. The scent was buried under other odors. Carefully she sorted out Avaliks from snowy owl, wolverine, and ground squirrel. Then, using it like a string, she followed the Avalik scent to the whelping den.

The flowers above the entrance had gone to seed, and the nearby redpoll nests were empty and frayed by the wind. The den's commanding view of the vast tundra was a wolf's dream, and Ice Blink lay down to rest.

The wind shifted and a leathery scent, mixed with smoke and whale blubber, drifted up from the riverbed. Ice Blink knew it well. A human was nearby—in fact, two humans. She slipped into the den and hid.

"Sometimes," said one of the two men, who were around the river bend sitting on a shoal, "sometimes the wolves come back to their dens at this time of year just to check them out. They like their dens, all right."

Ice Blink listened to the meaningless words.

"We've been here many sleeps," said the second man. "Do we really have to see a live wolf?"

"Yes, Steven Itta," said Peter Sugluk to his friend from Barrow. "We are The Wolf Dancers; we must have the spirit of the wolf in our feet. If we want to win the dance prize, we must watch the wolves to capture their spirit." He was silent as he thought. "We do want to win the Kivgiq dance award, don't we?"

"You want to," Steven Itta said, "so you can be a hero in Julie's eyes, and you and she can get married."

"I wish that was so, all right," replied Peter.

Then he was silent. Marriage wasn't a simple matter. Gone were the days when the Eskimos could live off the land without the help of modern technology—radios and refrigerators and electric light bulbs. To get those things, one needed a job that paid money, and these jobs were in the gussak's—the white man's—world. To get gussak jobs, one needed a gussak education, and that cost money.

Steven Itta also had been thinking during the silence. "It is too bad," he finally said, "that the Kivgiq does not give money for prizes. How are you going to go to college if you have only dancing feet?"

"I am not only a dancer; I am a very fast runner, Steven. The Fourth of July Foot Race pays lots of money. I have signed up for it already. I will win gussak money and do what I must in this new Arctic world. But I will keep on dancing. Dancing is our culture. I want to keep our traditions alive. Do I want too much, all right?"

The two young men sat quietly. Like their families and friends, they thought a long time before answering questions.

"The Arctic has gotten very complicated, all right," said Steven. "We cannot live as our ancestors did even if we want to."

"And I do," answered Peter Sugluk longingly. "With Julie I have watched the brotherhood of the wolves, and we have wished we were one with them again."

"That world is gone," said Steven Itta.

"Ee-lie," whispered Peter. "Get down on all fours. I smell wolf."

"All fours?"

"They don't know what you are when you're on all fours. When they see you standing on two legs, they know you're a human and they run away. But on all fours they don't know. Sometimes they come right up to find out."

They knelt with their hands on the ground for almost an hour. When Ice Blink did not appear, they began to talk again in their low, musical voices.

"Since we've been watching Julie's wolf pups for many circles of the sun," Steven Itta said, "we should be good enough wolf dancers by now. We saw how they wrestle with bones and hides and how they chase their tails. That is their spirit, all right."

"We are not pups," Peter answered. "We are adult wolves. We are regal, elegant, full of the sense of the Earth and our work upon it. A pup dance won't do."

Peter, silent now, pointed with his eyes to the top of the embankment.

As if struck into being, a white wolf stared at them. Her eyes were mustard yellow. She tilted her head curiously from right to left, trying to make sense of the strange animals lumped by the river. Although she smelled humans, these four-legged beasts were not humans in her mind. She reared onto her hind feet to see them better. Then, like a gyrfalcon's shadow, she came down the slope sniffing and rotating her ears to learn more about them. She hesitated, crouched low, still uncertain of what they were, and trotted to within fifteen feet of them. She stared quietly; then Steven sneezed and his human face became clear to her. She leaped, turned in midair, and sped away.

"I've got it," said Peter when she had disappeared in the tundra mist. Rising, he stamped out the rhythm of the Eskimo man dancer. He spread his feet, bent his knees, and with hands and body told the story of a wolf approaching a strange object that became a human. He even leaped and turned in midair, eyes round with fear.

"Teach me, teach me," said Steven Itta.

On the lonely beach beyond the bleak bend in the Arctic river, with the ice mist playing around their feet and bright-blue skies above, two young men danced the dance of "White Wolf Running from Two Men."

By the time they were satisfied with their art, Ice Blink was far down the scented Avalik highway that led to Kangik. The ambrosia of the wolf pack grew continuously stronger as she ran. She threaded along it, then suddenly came upon Silver. The rime-gray female was curled in a tight knot on the lichens below the crest of a rise. Ice Blink drew back. She had not been invited to trespass on this wolf's property. She whimpered her apology. The wolf did not move. After a long wait Ice Blink took one step toward her, then another. The wolf smelled cold. Ice Blink touched her with her nose. There was no life in the body.

She backed away and lay down a short distance from Silver, her nose on her paws, her eyes on the dead female. After a while she dozed.

Suddenly she was awake. The Avaliks were standing in a circle around her. Ice Blink lowered her ears in humility, at the same time making wolf judgments as she rolled her eyes from wolf to wolf. One female carried food in her mouth—a kind wolf, Aaka. Her daughter was constantly sniffing—a sensitive wolf, Sweet Fur Amy. One was disgruntled, Raw Bones. Then Ice Blink saw the alpha. He was larger than the others, and his fur stood up on his back and head like a regal cape. He was wolf nobility. She groveled toward him, her belly almost on the ground. She turned her eyes away from his to say he was leader. Then, in humility, she looked at him and begged for admission into the pack.

Kapu read her application. She was older than he, far from home, and alone. She was strong and well fed—a good hunter. One odor worried him. It was a sickly odor. That was enough to cast doubt. He turned his head away and refused her admission.

The Avaliks milled restlessly as they watched her retreat. Then Aaka dropped the food she was carrying and barked an alarm. She had found Silver's lifeless body.

Kapu howled. Sweet Fur Amy howled, Zing howled, Aaka howled, and Raw Bones moaned. The

Nuka adolescents lay down and put their heads on their paws. In silence they listened to the windlike voices of the Avaliks slide up the musical scale and glide down to silence. The life of Silver had fled.

When their mourning was over, Kapu led his wolves away. Silver was now part of the wilderness. She would enter the lives of the ravens and foxes, the lemmings and wolverines.

That rosy midnight, subdued by the loss of the old alpha female, the Avaliks gathered together on a desolate frost heave. Some stretched out on their sides and closed their eyes. Some watched the birds. Kapu watched the caribou on the horizon. The animals were behaving oddly. They were pressed tightly against each other. They were not spaced apart as usual. Then Kapu heard a high-pitched whine. Billions of mosquitoes and botflies were darkening the sky. They sought out the caribou. With no tails to whisk off the pests, the caribou were using the mass of their bodies as a fort. This was a problem for the wolves. It was going to be hard for them to isolate one or two.

Kapu was pondering a strategy when, over the sound of the pitiful bleats and snorts of the caribou, Sweet Fur Amy passed a message to him: "Time to go for the pups." Kapu arose, and the two trekked off through a massive cloud of insects. They swished them away with their tails and snapped at them. A few mosquitoes lit on the furless parts of their eyelids and noses, but they wiped them away with their paws. The dense underfur of the wolves protected their bodies.

They were just out of sight of the Avaliks when Raw Bones suddenly jumped out of the blueberries and landed on Kapu's back. Kapu reacted quickly. He clenched Raw Bones's shoulder in his jaws and twisted him to the ground. Once again Raw Bones bowed to Kapu's might and cringed before him. Head high, Kapu felt his own confidence rise. Raw Bones, in spite of himself, was making Kapu more and more powerful.

When Ice Blink, who had been watching them from some distance away, saw Raw Bones go down, she sensed it was time to take up her cause again. Silver was dead. Raw Bones was an annoyance to the leader. She caught up with Kapu and Sweet Fur Amy and followed them at a respectful distance. Kapu was immediately aware of her. Before he reached Kangik, he turned and waited, his back bristling. She walked into his personal tolerance zone and stopped. He stared at her. Silver was dead. The caribou were a formidable mass. He needed another wolf. With a soft

whine and an unblinking look he invited Ice Blink—
a biological time bomb—into the Avalik Pack.

A brief sense of uneasiness swept through him;
then Sweet Fur Amy whimpered to remind him of
their mission, and the three trotted on. They climbed
to the knoll and looked down on the scene Amy had
smelled and responded to. Willow Pup Julie and the
little boy, Amaroq, were outside on the riverbank.
The boy was laughing and romping with the wolf
pups.

Signaling Ice Blink to stay and Sweet Fur Amy to
follow, Kapu swept down on Uqaq. He picked her up
by the scruff of her neck. She instinctively curled her
body into the pup-carrying position, with her hind
feet curled up to her head. She was almost too big to
be carried. Her rump bumped the ground. Kapu
lifted his head higher and trotted off with her.

Sweet Fur Amy picked up Nutik. He was even
bigger and heavier than Uqaq, and she could not
carry him. She dragged him along.

"Amy," Julie said when she saw what was happening. "Not yet. Don't take Nutik. Don't take Uqaq.
Not yet. They need shots. Qignak from Canada has
tracked a rabid wolf to our tundra. It carries a deadly
disease." Sweet Fur Amy tugged, slowly moving toward Ice Blink, who was coming to help her.

"Wolves must not die," Julie whispered as she came toward Amy. "You manage the tundra, the caribou, the berries, the birds, the plants—all the wild things we need." She dropped to her knees and reached out for Nutik. Ice Blink leaped away. Amy pulled harder.

"Amy, stay. Stay. The veterinarian is coming to Kangik to give the dogs and your pups rabies shots. I will bring them to you after that, all right. Do not take the pups."

Amaroq, seeing Julie on all fours, thought she was playing wolf and climbed on her back. He tumbled her to her side, and she could not reach Nutik.

"Drop, Amy. Drop," she called, and barked an alarm. Sweet Fur Amy stopped.

"Drop," Julie said, and reached out to gently hold Sweet Fur Amy's nose in her hand. She shook it in the manner of the alpha male wolf saying he is boss. Sweet Fur Amy dropped Nutik. The big fuzzy pup looked from Sweet Fur Amy to Julie, then ran to Julie, the only mother he remembered.

Sweet Fur Amy barked at him, demanding he come with her. He ignored her.

"Not now, Amy," Willow Pup Julie said. "I will soon return him to you, all right." She gathered Nutik up in her arms. He licked her cheek.

Peter Sugluk came around the far side of the house, his leather pants swishing softly, the weasel tails on his boots swinging with the rhythm of his stride. His dark, lean face was serious as he sat down on the ground beside Julie.

"I heard you talking to Amy," he said. "I know you want to give the pups rabies shots, but somehow wolves know how to control the disease. Not many die of it."

"That is true," she answered. "The wolves know, all right. But we don't know how they do it, and we cannot take a chance. Dr. Flossie Oomittuk says there are too many people and dogs hunting on the tundra. She asked me to give the pups shots."

Sweet Fur Amy stopped to listen to Peter's and Willow Pup Julie's voices and to the boy who was playing pounce with Nutik. Nutik snarled.

"No, no," Amaroq said. "Don't get mad." The snarls stopped.

"Good, Nutik. Good pup," Willow Pup Julie said, and she and Peter took Nutik and the little boy into the house.

Sweet Fur Amy had seen that Nutik had a human alpha, a little boy with a kind voice. But she would not give up. She lay down in a patch of dwarf peas to wait until the pup came out to play.

Kapugen's voice reached her from inside the house.

"Uqaq is gone?" he said. "That is too bad, all right. She was a lovely pup."

"We must return Nutik soon," Julie said.

"Return him? I do not agree. I need him. He is a strong leader and he is friendly. The greatest dogs come from such a wolf."

"But I promised the wolves I would bring him back," she said.

"Ee-lie, Miyax," Kapugen said, calling Julie by her Yupik Eskimo name. "Think, my little panIk, my daughter. The village will have a new industry—sled dogs with the friendliness and endurance of the wolf. That means money for the things we need."

"The caribou need Nutik," Julie said softly. "The grasses and lichens need Nutik. The birds and mammals need Nutik. And we need them all."

The father and daughter stopped talking. When they disagreed, they turned inward to think. Finally Kapugen broke the silence.

"I want my son to learn the strength and wisdom of the wolf from young Nutik," he said.

Willow Pup Julie did not answer.

Sweet Fur Amy waited for the pup she was responsible for to come out of the house. Presently the villagers came outside, and she trotted the several miles upriver to the pack.

They were standing around Uqaq looking at her with curiosity. The pup held her tail between her legs, her ears back, her eyes cast down. Although Uqaq knew she was among her kind, she was waiting for her human mother to tell her what to do. She did not know Raw Bones was her father, nor did he feel very parental. She was too big, the size of an independent pup.

On the other hand, Sweet Fur Amy's baby-sitting instincts sharpened. The pup was frightened and helpless. She licked the pup's cheeks and ears. Uqaq relaxed in this tenderness and sank to her belly. Sweet Fur Amy lay beside her and licked her so hard, the pup fell onto her side. Sweet Fur Amy went on licking. When she had removed the people scent, she rubbed her own Avalik scent on her. Then she got up and woofed. Uqaq followed her baby-sitter to the Avaliks' last kill.

Sweet Fur Amy's world was in order at last. She had a pup to tend. Slowly Uqaq would shift her love for her human mother to her baby-sitter.

When the sun dipped toward the horizon, then started up again, Uqaq and Sweet Fur Amy were curled side by side near the pack.

Hardly had they closed their eyes than Storm Call lay down beside Sweet Fur Amy. He liked her. In fact, he had liked her from the moment she had herded him into the pack. She wagged her tail once.

Raw Bones stayed away from the Avaliks until Ice Blink settled down; then he curled up beside her. She snarled, got up, and lay down near Aaka. Aaka snarled and went to Kapu's side. Lichen whimpered because her brother had left her for Sweet Fur Amy. Zing heard her protest and took sides with her. He rumbled at Storm Call.

Kapu listened to the restless whimpers and shifting arrangements. This was not the first time he had noticed that his pack was breaking up into cliques. Sweet Fur Amy had isolated herself with Uqaq and Storm Call. Zing and Lichen barked at them, and all of them stayed away from Ice Blink. Raw Bones rumbled alone.

Kapu got to his feet. This was not good. A pack must cooperate. The time had come for him to lead them on another long trip around their territory. A pack's land—the herds, the plants, the weather, and the winding rivers—binds wolves together. Trips across and around their land fill each individual with a sense of his importance to the pack and the pack to him. It was time to fuse the Avaliks into a more friendly nation. He would lead them off as soon as the night was long enough for them to travel great distances in the dark, which they preferred to the light.

That day came in September after the first snow fell. Kapu was dozing when, with his head on his tail, he heard the subtle call to winter travel. A wooly bear caterpillar was walking down the tines of the moss beneath him. The fuzzy brown-and-black larva was so cold, he could no longer eat. He was going to the warmest layer on the frigid tundra—the inch or two of atmosphere right against the ground. Here the caterpillar would freeze for the winter but not die. Next summer he would thaw and eat until the cold stopped him again. Fourteen years of freezing and thawing would pass before the caterpillar would become an adult tiger moth. It takes only three weeks in the lower forty-eight states. Kapu heard the caterpillar stop creeping. It was time to go.

He stood up, shook sparklets of rime from his fur, and howled the Avalik song of travel. The wolves awoke and got to their feet. Aaka howled, Zing harmonized with her, then Storm Call came from his rendezvous and joined in. Eager to please her new alpha, Lichen howled half tones that quivered the air. Kapu wagged his tail and stepped closer to Aaka.

The spirit of the gypsy howl touched Ice Blink. She howled. Raw Bones took his own note and bellowed authoritatively. The wolves sang, sending their glorious music out over the land—all but Sweet Fur Amy and Uqaq. They were not going to travel. They listened to the song and dug their noses deeper into their tails.

The howl ended when Kapu's deepest note faded away. The Avaliks touched noses, cheeks, shoulders and milled in joyful anticipation of the long run.

Kapu burst free. The pack followed, feet flying, tails loose and out, fur sweeping back and rippling.

When Raw Bones realized they were not going to the Colville River, he broke off from the pack. Ice Blink followed him. Kapu glanced at them as they headed south. For deep reasons of survival he did not understand, he was relieved to see Ice Blink go.

Rid of them both, he led on with renewed inspiration. The Avaliks covered almost ten miles in less than an hour. Near a frost heave they picked up the trail of a grizzly bear, sped off to find him, and chased him for the fun of it. Then they circled back to their own trail and ran on.

The chase gave Raw Bones time to change his mind and catch up with them. Ice Blink trotted beside him. Kapu saw the two return, and his spirits darkened. He increased his pace. Zing sensed trouble. He left Lichen's side and ran behind Kapu, putting his feet precisely in his footsteps. Storm Call ran third to support his alpha.

Suddenly Raw Bones passed him and caught up with Zing. Unruffled, Zing put on speed and kept ahead of Raw Bones. Then Aaka passed all three and took her honored place with the alpha male. Ice Blink took up the rear. This pack was not at ease with her. She would keep her distance. It had been seven months since her mate had died and she had licked saliva from his face. She had no knowledge of the death bomb she was carrying, but she did know she needed this pack to survive.

Although she was not fond of Raw Bones, the troublemaker, he was necessary to her. Without him and his friends she would not survive. The winters were long and hard, and the caribou and moose dangerous. Ice Blink caught up with Raw Bones and ran by his side. He glanced at her, raised the base of his tail, and let his handsome bush hang loose in the friendly position. To Ice Blink this was acceptance. They were a team.

Before dawn Kapu brought the pack to a resting site and took Zing off to study a bull caribou. The animal was covered with infections where the botflies and mosquitoes had bitten. He limped. Kapu and Zing looked at each other and nonchalantly walked to within a few hundred yards of the bull. The bull kept a wary eye on them. The pack lay on their bellies and watched. After a long while the bull decided the two wolves were not hunting him and leaned down to browse. Kapu signaled Zing to attack. The bull saw the signal and trotted off. Raw Bones and Ice Blink ran in to help. Lichen and Storm Call closed in behind, and Aaka circled out to herd the animal. She would head the bull toward them. Wolves stay clear of the kicking rear feet.

Illness and strategy notwithstanding, the buck thundered away behind a screen of frozen mist. But the wolves did not stop running. Without losing a step, they used their noses and ears to follow the prey. Shoulders pumping up and down, tails flowing, they saw him again, rushed at him, but could not catch up. The Avaliks sorely missed Sweet Fur Amy. They trotted on.

Two days later the food was finally won. They ate their fill and retired to the top of a small rise, where they could look in all directions night and day. By night they saw with the aid of the light-gathering rods in their eyes. The cones gave them daytime vision. Night and day were of no concern to the wolves.

A helicopter clattered into the morning sunshine. Kapu feared machines whether they came by land or air. He aroused the pack with one woofbark and raced to the top of a cliff above the Lower Colville River valley. There Aaka took the lead. She had grown up in this area and knew all the overhangs and gullies. The helicopter followed her. She turned abruptly and vanished. The pack zigged, zagged, and joined her beneath an overhang on a creek embankment.

"Lost them," said Dr. Flossie Oomittuk, the North Slope Borough veterinarian, who was seated by the pilot of the helicopter.

"Want to land and find them?" asked Jeremy Smith as he steered the copter toward the river. "They're around here somewhere."

"The pack's too big for the two of us to tranquilize them all. Let's go back for help. They'll stick around. Some of the caribou haven't gone south yet."

The pilot nodded and swung the clattering machine in an arc. Flossie Oomittuk spoke again.

"Who told you a big white female ran west after her whole pack died of rabies?"

"Qignak," the pilot answered.

"Qignak. He should know. He's the Inuttut Eskimo who first reported the rabid pack."

"He knew them well," said the pilot. "He's lived in their territory all his life. He said the big white female with the long pointed nose survived. He tracked her over the Canadian border into Alaska. He has seen her from time to time. He flies over this country when he's counting caribou to help our Fish and Game Department. Think she's carrying the disease?"

"She's certainly a candidate," said Dr. Oomittuk. "But so far no rabies has turned up on the North Slope, and it's been almost four months since she entered. Of course, the incubation period can be as long as a year."

"What's the point of inoculating wolves against rabies?" the pilot asked. "The less wolves, the more caribou."

"The reason is people," the veterinarian said. "Rabies is deadly. We can inoculate a few people against it—vets, wildlife researchers, and people who work with dogs and wild animals—but it's not practical to inoculate whole human populations. It's more practical to inoculate dogs, cats, foxes, and wolves when we can."

"Come to think of it," Jeremy said, "I did see a large white wolf in that pack we just lost."

"I noticed one too," said Flossie Oomittuk.

"Are you sure they'll stay around here until we get back?"

"I think so," the veterinarian said. "That's a fresh kill at the headwaters of the creek. Fly back over it. Let's get its location on the Global Positioning System and come back."

The copter flew over the kill, circled several times, and went on.

When it was no longer audible to even the keen-eared wolves, who could hear a caribou tendon click a half mile away, Raw Bones got up and started out for the kill. Kapu intercepted him, ears straight up and forward, brow wrinkled. "No." Raw Bones stopped and Kapu bounced on his hind feet, took a long leap, and ran southwest. Raw Bones looked in the direction of the kill, hesitated, and joined the run. Kapu was headed toward his territory.

But Kapu did not go to the Upper Colville. He led the pack day and night, checking borders, harvesting food, howling to distant packs. He ran until the sun no longer rose and the air and the land were shades of blue and white and the northern lights made the snowy world almost as bright as daytime.

One night he lost Ice Blink. The older wolf could not keep up with the swift pace of the young alpha. Kapu put on more speed. He had an urgent need to lose Ice Blink, but not for any clear reason. She did her part, she stayed the omega, the helpless, so he could not drive her off or kill her. But he sensed he had to lose her. Then, fortunately, when she could no longer keep up, Raw Bones dropped back to be with her.

By the twilight of noon the next day Kapu and the Avaliks were racing free of anxiety. They were kicking up snow with their heels, playing wolf jokes on little herds of musk oxen.

When they had traveled almost two hundred miles, Kapu brought the pack to the den on the Avalik River. They wagged their tails, rubbed bodies, and licked each other. Fellowship reigned. The Avaliks howled their anthem proudly and carried their banner of scent.

From across the freezing landscape Sweet Fur Amy answered, then Uqaq. Kapu bounced up and down and called back. They talked over the long distance, letting each other know where they were, but neither moving. Sweet Fur Amy was not coming home.

She and Uqaq were watching the village. The people of Kangik were outdoors in the bright moonlight getting their sleds and snow machines ready for moose hunts under the new sun in January. Kapu called to her again. This time she did not answer.

Amaroq and Nutik were alone on the riverbank.

Sweet Fur Amy sent a high call note to Nutik: "Come here." It was so high the boy could not hear it. Nutik heard it, but it meant nothing to him. The boy and his family were his pack, and he heard only their commands. The toddler ran toward the ice-filled river. Nutik pulled him back by his big, warm parka. Amaroq laughed. The two woofed and whimpered the wolf sounds of best friends.

Nutik did not answer Sweet Fur Amy, but Kapu did. He called her to come back and hunt with them. The bulk of the herd had migrated to the forest to breed and renew life. Kapu needed her keen nose to locate the scattered winter herds. He called her again.

She did not answer. The northern lights were illuminating the green house. Its door was opening. Willow Pup Julie walked out. She cupped her hands around her mouth and howled to Amy, as she had every day during these long dark months. "I am here. I am here," she had always said, and Sweet Fur Amy had always answered, "Here am I waiting for the pup." Today Willow Pup Julie's wolf call was different. It was low with sadness. Sweet Fur Amy came closer.

"Amy," Willow Pup Julie said when she could

make out her shadow, "I cannot return Nutik. I have kept him too long. He is a member of our pack. He cannot and will not leave."

Amy listened.

"I am sorry," Julie went on. "We will love Nutik and learn from him." Amy did not understand the words, but her wolf eyes saw well by the green and yellow lights of the aurora. The girl's body was speaking. She was saying in gesture and pose, "I am sorry, the pup is not yours anymore."

Sweet Fur Amy threw back her head and sang about a wolf pup lost to humans. It was not a sad cry. It was a thoughtful song inspired by the distant past. Long before there were domestic dogs, people raised friendly wolf pups. The people and wolves had much in common. They were both social animals who hunted big game. They both lived in family groups. Both groups had leaders and shared a deep love for these alphas. When humans saw what good hunters the wolves were, they took the most friendly pups into their families, and the wolf pups came to love the human alphas as they loved their own. Over the eons friendly wolf pups were bred to other friendly wolf pups, and the dog evolved in its various shapes and sizes. Even today a wolf pup who is taken from its parents very early in life will substitute the human

alphas for its own. And that is what Julie was telling Sweet Fur Amy.

Sweet Fur Amy understood. She went back to Uqaq and led her to a distant sleeping spot. They lay with their heads on their paws listening to the sighs of blowing snow and the boom of river ice freezing deeper as the temperature dropped to forty below zero.

The northern lights faded, and the stars shone down on the icy snowflakes and lit up the tundra. Sweet Fur Amy heard Aklaq, the grizzly bear, and she tucked her paws against her belly fur. The bear was sighing. Sweet Fur Amy lifted her head. In the starlight she saw Aklaq sitting upright on an embankment of drifted snow. A wolf hunter had landed his noisy plane on the river ice. Aklaq awakened. Although she was in her winter sleep, she could arouse herself if she must. She struggled sleepily from her den and ran.

A hunter got out of his plane and walked across the creaking cold snow. A dart gun was slung across his shoulder. He circled the Avalik den, saw no bear sign, and went back to his plane. He took off.

Aklaq went back to her den. She sat down. Her big shoulders were slumped, her head drooped. Her cubs of four years were on their own. In a warmer climate where food is more abundant, grizzly cubs leave their mothers when they are two years old, but in the food-scarce Arctic it takes more years to learn the resources. Cubless in August, Aklaq had mated with a boar grizzly of the Lower Colville River. She would give birth in January.

Now she was sensing the three atmospheric signals that were telling her she would be safe if she went back into her den. The air pressure was dropping. That was one signal for Aklaq. The cold intensified. That was a second signal. The stars went out and storm clouds blackened the land. Aklaq got to her feet. She lumbered past a weasel who was plugging his den with moss against the coming blizzard. She passed a wolverine digging into a burrow near a sleeping ground squirrel colony. She smelled the ptarmigan who were hunkered down in the grass waiting to be buried under a blanket of snow that would keep them warm. They all felt the storm coming.

The wolves felt it too, but reacted differently. The Nuka River Pack howled in celebration of a storm that would pile snow high and slow down the caribou. The Avaliks sang to the wind that would pack the snow as hard as cement and set them free to run on top of it. The Lower Colville River Pack ran out in the storm to hunt moose, who could not run in this weather, and the Mountain Pack trotted into the forest to locate the young caribou who would not have the strength to run in deep snow. They all howled to welcome the blizzard.

At midnight the storm hit. That was the third signal. As Aklaq went into her den, the blowing snow wiped out her footsteps so no human hunter would know where she slept.

The weasel was inspired. He began digging a tunnel under the snow to a lemming nest. The ptarmigan grew warm.

Sweet Fur Amy and Uqaq dove in and out of the snow, rolling in it, biting it. They barked the delight woof of the wolf.

Suddenly on the wind came a delight answer. Sweet Fur Amy peered through the swirling whiteness. Storm Call was coming through the blizzard carrying a polished caribou tine in his mouth. He dropped it in the snow at Sweet Fur Amy's feet. She wagged her tail and picked it up. She tossed it. Storm Call caught it. Sweet Fur Amy chased him, took the tine in her mouth, and pulled hard. Growling and swishing their tails, they played tug-of-war in the whirling snow while Uqaq tumbled and watched.

The storm raged for three days before it blew south to the Brooks Mountain Range. When it passed, the stars burned brightly, and by their light the Sweet Fur Clique ran until they came to the land between the Meade and Ikpikpuk rivers. There they bedded down near a small herd of resident caribou spending the winter on the North Slope.

The Sweet Fur Clique worked well together. Amy found the weak animals, and Uqaq annoyed them with her ooing and woofing until they turned to charge her. Then Storm Call would give the signal to attack. Sometimes he did not. He had good judgment. He knew when to call off a chase and when to drive on. He knew when to rest and when to run. They lived well in the land between the rivers.

The joy of being with Storm Call and Uqaq, hunting and diving in the snow, helped Sweet Fur Amy forget about the lost Nutik. When the sun came above the horizon in January, the Sweet Fur Clique was fat and spirited. They wandered, chased each other in circles, and rolled in the snow.

Near the Colville early one morning, Sweet Fur Amy stopped and sniffed. Storm Call and Uqaq stopped. On the air was the scent of Willow Pup Julie. She was nearby. Sweet Fur threw back her head and called to her. Julie called back. Silence, then a creak of sled runners, and over a rise came Nutik pulling Amaroq in the one-dog sled and Julie running beside them.

Uqaq ran to her brother.

"Stop," barked Sweet Fur Amy, but Uqaq could not. She was too excited. She leaped on Nutik. He twisted her off, pulling the harness and overturning the sled with Amaroq. The little boy rolled into the snow, his laughter muffled in a pile of cold crystals. Nutik dug around him, yip-barking for the fun of it all.

Amaroq stood up. Nutik pranced. "Stop," the boy barked, and Nutik stopped. Uqaq whimpered, begging him to play, but Nutik did not move. His leader had spoken. Uqaq sat down and cocked her head from right to left.

Willow Pup Julie straightened out the tangled traces and put Amaroq back in the sled. Then she came toward Sweet Fur Amy whimpering wolf niceties. There was love and authority in Julie's voice. Sweet Fur Amy got down on her belly. Uqaq got down. Suddenly, with a move as swift as a falcon's strike, Julie jabbed a hypodermic needle into Amy's thigh and then quickly into Uqaq's. There was no pain, but the wolves were so startled by Julie's jumping at them that they ran quite a distance before they stopped and looked at her.

"Forgive me, Amy," Willow Pup Julie said. "I have no way of telling you this, but there is a rabid wolf on the tundra. I have given you a vaccine so you will not get sick and die." Then she saw Storm Call standing on the snow pile. She crept toward him. "Come," she whimpered in wolf talk. "I want to be your friend." He had seen Sweet Fur and Uqaq run away from Julie, so he was cautious.

"Bring me your friend, Amy," Julie said softly. "I must give him a shot too." The three wolves stood motionless, staring at her.

Then Storm Call barked danger and ran off. Sweet Fur Amy and Uqaq ran after him. Julie pushed a glossy strand of her black hair under her parka hood.

"Amy," she called, "where is Kapu?" The trio kept running, and Julie returned to the sled.

"Hut," Amaroq said to Nutik, and they moved on.

Kapu was several miles away, loping toward the Upper Colville River with his pack. He was in a fine mood. Raw Bones and Ice Blink were gone. Sweet Fur Amy and Storm Call were on their own with Uqaq, and the Avaliks had stopped feuding. Good feeling prevailed. It had come through their feet as they ran. It had come through their eyes and noses as they learned where each fox and rabbit lived and each group of overwintering caribou. It had come through their bodies as they pierced the snowstorms with the ease of a salmon swimming upstream. Kapu jogged along, head high, spirits elevated. He was, at last, a great alpha.

The Avaliks threaded their way across the snowy wilderness in perfect harmony. They moved as one, vanishing into snow clouds and reappearing in spotlights of yellow sunshine.

As they approached the Upper Colville River, Raw Bones suddenly sprang out of a clump of dwarf willows and dashed to the head of the pack. Kapu ignored him. Feeling the power of being in first place, Raw Bones snarled and growled gloriously. Kapu did not return the challenge.

When he was tired of Raw Bones's nonsense, he simply expanded his chest and sped past him. Raw Bones bared his teeth. Kapu turned and faced him. "I am the alpha," he said, posturing regally. Raw Bones pulled his ears back and down, and not only lowered himself but rolled over on his back. He flashed the wolf flag of surrender—the white belly fur. Kapu cocked an eye at him. Never before had Raw Bones taken this pose of complete defeat. Was he at last subdued? It seemed so. He let him up. Raw Bones slunk away with his tail between his legs.

Kapu turned to Aaka, licked her cheek, and took a long high leap, and the two ran toward the river. Beside them ran Zing and Lichen.

Near the frozen Colville Kapu stopped. Sensing something was not right, he looked back. Raw Bones had returned to the pack and brought Ice Blink with him.

A searing bolt of fear ran through Kapu. All his instincts told him to drive off the white wolf. Then Aaka called him. A moose was in the valley. Devotion to his mate won over fear, and he joined her. Raw Bones and Ice Blink followed well behind, but part of the pack.

Ice Blink stumbled. She stopped, wiped a watering eye against her foreleg, then caught up with Raw Bones. She whimpered in pain. Whatever had bothered Kapu now bothered Raw Bones. He dashed away to catch up with the pack.

They raced over their old border and into what had once had been the no-wolf zone between Kapu's and Raw Bones's territories. They ran through the dwarf alders and grasses to the other side of the river and into Raw Bones's empty territory.

An odor struck Kapu like a sharp fang, and he jerked to a stop. The fur rose on his back. Eyes wide, he gave a silent signal and turned his pack around.

Not Raw Bones. He wanted to be king again. He walked through the stunted brush and up an incline to his old whelping den. He would return to his beloved land and regain his self-confidence. He lay down and put his head on his paws. As he sighed a peaceful sigh, Ice Blink appeared. Her eye had stopped watering. She drooped her head wearily, then lay down to rest.

It was March. The wolf mating season was beginning, the season that marked a new year for the wolves. Although wolf pairs stay close together all year—in fact, all their lives—they mate only once a year. This year, with Aaka in good health, Kapu could expect lots of fat pups.

Ice Blink as well as Aaka was coming into estrus. She was not ready to mate quite yet, but she was willing to be courted. One night she ran to Raw Bones and spanked her front feet on the snow, asking him to play. He bounced to her. She wagged her tail and ran. Raw Bones ran. As they came around a cluster of stunted spruce trees, he was suddenly struck a powerful blow on his rear. He was spun completely around.

Snow Driver, the alpha male of the Mountain Pack, had hit him with a rump blow, and before Raw Bones could recover, he had him by the scruff of his neck. Cloud Berry, the alpha female, rolled Ice Blink to her back. Seven other handsome gray wolves surrounded them.

The powerful Mountain Pack had taken over Raw Bones's old territory. The riverside was his home no more. He cowered before Snow Driver, waiting for the Avaliks to come to his rescue.

They did not. A deep draft of moist air had told Kapu what Raw Bones had discovered the hard way—that Snow Driver and his pack now owned this land. Kapu had smelled the news, crossed the river, and returned to his own territory. He scent marked the border, once again setting up the no-wolf zone.

On the south side of the river in view of the Mountain Pack, Ice Blink suddenly went stiff. Her eyes rolled, foam bubbled from her mouth. She snarled.

Cloud Berry looked at her. A defeated wolf did not growl at the conqueror. Ice Blink had threatened her with a growl. The white wolf staggered to her feet and, lunging, sank her aching teeth in Cloud Berry's front leg. Snow Driver rushed in to defend Cloud Berry. He postured like an alpha, but Ice Blink did not roll onto her back. It was as if she had not seen him. Something was wrong. With a tail command he sent Cloud Berry up the mountain into the taiga, ice-dwarfed spruce trees. Then he turned back to the business of dominating Ice Blink. As she snarled toward him, mouth open, he smelled the sickness, turned, and followed Cloud Berry.

When he was gone, Raw Bones slowly got to his feet. He glanced at Ice Blink. She was on the ground stiff with paralysis. Fear gripped him again and he ran. Crossing the Colville, he slithered up to the top of the embankment, where he lay down with his tail between his legs.

Within a few hours Ice Blink went into convulsions and died the horrible death of the rabid animal, wracked with pain, wanting but unable to swallow water, and blinded by headache and fever. She had carried the disease for more than a year before it had taken over. And she had contaminated the Mountain Pack before she died.

On their side of the river the Avaliks urinated and howled to tell the Mountain Pack where their border lay. The Mountain Pack howled back from the taiga. Storm Driver acknowledged the rights of Kapu, leader of the Avaliks, and Kapu acknowledged Storm Driver as leader of the Mountain Pack. With howls and scratches on the snow they defined the no-wolf corridor.

That night the Avaliks started back toward Kangik. In the quiet of the blue twilight after the sun went down, Kapu and Aaka mated.

Pups! And they would be the alphas' pups.

Pups! Far away, Sweet Fur Amy heard the news and led Storm Call and Uqaq across the tundra back to the Avaliks. Before she reached them, she picked up the scent of a caribou weakened by infection, and the three easily and swiftly felled it. Their quick harmonious howls announced the kill. Sweet Fur Amy ate first.

Kapu, Aaka, Zing, Lichen, and Raw Bones heard the news and joined the feast. Kapu let Aaka eat before him, making sure she would give birth to many healthy Avalik pups. When Aaka could swallow no more, Kapu ate and generously permitted the others to eat with him. Their bellies round with food, they milled and mixed scents and celebrated their good fortune. Then they made sleeping beds.

Sweet Fur Amy, Storm Call, and Uqaq made their beds with them. The alphas' pups were coming. They would stay with the pack and help. Uqaq found a bone toy and took it to bed with her.

As old as she was, almost a year, Uqaq was still a puppy. The many mothers in her life—Silver, Julie, and Sweet Fur Amy—had kept her from growing up. She was stuck in puppyhood, a sweet playful pack member who could not contribute much to the survival of the group. She was Sweet Fur Amy's and Storm Call's welfare case. With their return to the Avaliks she was everyone's welfare case. Uqaq needed a kindly pack to keep her alive.

A March blizzard covered the sleeping wolves that morning, and from time to time Kapu awoke, shook off the snow, and listened to the sounds of the tundra. A human voice traveled to him.

"Peter," said Willow Pup Julie. Kapu lifted his head. "There are the wolves. See the ears above the snow? They are sleeping. Kapu is awake."

"He's a prince," Peter whispered softly. Shifting on his caribou skin, he lifted his binoculars to his eyes.

"Be very quiet," Willow Pup Julie murmured.

The hours passed. The wolves knew Julie and Peter were there but they were not concerned. Too full to move, they went on sleeping off their huge meal. Later they got up, exchanged scents, mingled and licked cheeks. With the Sweet Fur Clique back among them, their society was nicely balanced—four adults, three young adults, one yearling, and pups on the way. The Avaliks were peaceful.

Voices floated to them from the caribou skins.

"He's all nobility," Peter breathed softly. "I shall become him. I will dance as I have never danced before."

"But you have already won the Kivgiq," Julie whispered.

"I need to win next year, too," Peter whispered back. "Then I can tour the state and earn money. Living in Barrow and going to college is very expensive—especially when you can't hunt and fish."

The clatter of a helicopter sounded in the distance. Inside it people were talking.

"Ravens," said Jeremy Smith, the pilot. "There must be a wolf kill over there."

"Get in touch with Kapugen's party," said Flossie Oomittuk, the veterinarian. "He's on a moose hunt somewhere along the Upper Colville River. He should be ready to help us." She turned to two men in the back of the copter, Agiaq and Uvigaq, the best hunters in Barrow. "Check the tranquilizing drugs and the guns," she said.

After a few screeches and static on the radio Jeremy got Kapugen's CB.

"Have you seen Julie's wolves?" he asked.

"Julie and Peter are near them now," Kapugen said. "They are not far from that kill where the ravens are circling. Julie has a CB; you can talk to her."

"How long has she been there?" he asked.

"Hours."

"How many wolves?"

"Eight. Two have been given shots. The smaller of the two black wolves and a gray adolescent pup."

"Did Julie and Peter see the white wolf?"

"She is dead," replied Kapugen. "I found her on the other side of the river."

"That is good, all right," said Flossie Oomittuk.

"Do you still want to inoculate the others?" Kapugen asked.

"Yes," the vet answered. "We don't know how many she infected before she went down. They all need inoculations. Join Julie and Peter. We'll need all three of you to help. I am numbering the wolves and will assign each of them to one of us so we don't all shoot at the same wolf."

The copter circled far away from the wolves to give Kapugen time to cover the distance to Julie and Peter. He decided to ski to save time.

"While we've got them knocked out," Jeremy said to Flossie, "we could get the alpha male wolf for Dr. Hardy."

"What's he want an alpha for?" Flossie asked.

"He wants to observe the heart rates of a leader and a subordinate to see if the roles they play make any difference in stress on the heart."

"That's important research," said the vet.

"Why?" asked Agiaq, one of the dart-gun men.

"Animal studies tell us a lot about humans," Flossie answered. "It's pretty hard to put a president in a room with a subordinate and put monitors on their hearts, but wolves can give us insight. They have a society very much like our own. They have presidents and vice presidents, talented ones with rank and ne'er-do-wells with no rank—like we do."

"Seems like a leader sure wouldn't be nervous with an underling," said Agiaq.

"It does, but you don't know for sure until you run a scientific experiment," said the vet.

Jeremy looked down at the tundra. "It would be nice to get Dr. Hardy an alpha," he repeated. "He's a good man, and he's been trying to capture one for years. I'd like to help him."

"But the wolf is our brother," Agiaq said with controlled disapproval in his voice. "We hunt them, but we don't torment them."

"Julie," said Flossie Oomittuk, "do you hear me?"

"I hear you, Flossie. Kapugen is here with me and Peter. We are ready."

"We are going to land behind the wolves and shoot them with the tranquilizing drugs. They should run toward you. We will follow them in the copter and note where they fall. You find them and give them the shots.

"Are you ready? Out."

"We are ready. Out."

Jeremy came in low and set the craft gently down.

Each person in the copter took aim at a different wolf, and they pulled the triggers almost simultaneously.

Kapu felt the needle hit him, leaped to his feet, and ran full out in Julie's direction. The others ran when they were shot. Finally they slowed down and fell as the tranquilizing drug took effect. They slumped onto the snow in quiet sleep. The copter rose and came down near three of them.

"Julie," said Kapugen, "inoculate Kapu and the steel-gray one."

"That's Zing," she said.

"Peter, take the rime-gray and smaller black one."

"Aaka and Amy," said Julie. "Amy has had shots."

"Okay, Peter, take the rangy gray wolf, and the one next to him," said Kapugen.

"Raw Bones," Julie said. "The other is Uqaq— she's had her shots too."

Julie and Peter skied quickly to their wolves and inoculated them. Then they skied away, glancing back to see Flossie climb out of the copter and inoculate the last two wolves.

"That's all of them," Julie said. "My beautiful wolves will live."

"That's good, all right," said Peter, picking up the caribou skin and their packs. She and Peter skied back to Kapugen's moose-hunting camp.

"Someday," said Julie when she had closed the tent flaps and tied them, "I would like to find out how the wolves keep rabies from spreading. Flossie says it perplexes her. Whole populations of white foxes are wiped out, but not wolves."

"Maybe they tell each other to stay away from a rabid member of the pack," said Peter. "They are very intelligent."

"They are intelligent," said Julie softly. "I hope Kapu knows I am trying to help him. It is not very pleasant to be darted."

"He knows, all right," said Peter. "Wolves hear other voices."

On the tundra Kapu came out of a deep sleep. He staggered to his feet, lost his balance, and regained it. He blinked. Far away a helicopter clattered into the ether. He seemed to be alone. He scanned the landscape and waited. Presently Aaka stood up and stumbled to him. He licked her face and eyes and cheeks. Zing walked over a rise, shaking his head. One by one the Avaliks awoke and found their way to Kapu.

They sensed something had happened but had no memory of what it was.

Nervously they rubbed their scents on each other to regain their confidence and unity. Then Kapu pranced and wagged his tail, and they all played a game of chase.

"Wooooooo." From the far distance Willow Pup Julie's voice sang the "all's well" song of the wolf. Kapu stopped and let the message sink in. "All's well." Some danger was over. He pressed his big feet on the snow, and with tail relaxed, head high, he led his wolf pack toward the Avalik River.

A cloud dropped snow so dense they could not see. This did not slow their speed. They traveled on by sound and internal compasses. As they jogged along, the tranquilizing drugs wore off and were forgotten.

Pups were coming. Kapu's own pups. Tails swished as the wolf pack came down the embankment to the bench where the whelping den was dug.

Kapu watched a group of caribou in the distance; they moved north as they grazed on moss. The natural flow of the migration had been restored. Once more the females had come out of the mountain passes and crossed the Colville into Avalik land. The pups would be big and fat.

Aaka dug the snow from the den entrance and clawed her way into the chamber. Kapu watched her, his tail wagging. The others made wolf beds on the top of the embankment and looked out across the snowdrifts that were slowly melting in the longer hours of sunlight.

Three sleeps later they were on the move again, noting the thin and disabled herd members, checking the mosses and grasses where the herd would be likely to feed. From time to time they harvested a caribou, then ran again. Occasionally they circled past Kangik and stopped to watch Nutik lead Kapugen's sled dogs. He ran with his head up to say he was proud to be leader. He worked with enthusiasm.

On the first of June Aaka nudged Kapu. He jumped to his feet. Pups! He glanced at the pack and with his eyes signaled them to follow. They were wide awake, waiting to go. Kapu and Aaka took off for the den, tails wagging, mouths open in excitement. Pups!

In the rosy light cast by the midnight sun Aaka gave birth. The firstborn was a male, black and aggressive: Grappler.

Kapu stood at the den entrance until the seventh pup was born—seven fine, healthy pups! When Aaka was resting quietly, he signaled Sweet Fur Amy,

Storm Call, and Zing. They howled the pup-arrival song and raced off to hunt for Aaka.

A few miles beyond the den Kapu felt the ground shake. He knew the rhythm—caribou were stamping. Quietly, keeping low to the ground, he and his wolves stole within view of the panicking herd. A charging grizzly bear was chasing them.

Kapu saw his opportunity. The bear had the caribou's full attention. Kapu glanced at Sweet Fur Amy and sent a message to Zing and Storm Call, and all broke into a run. They sped into the herd, split off a group, and separated a calf from its mother. The bear saw the frightened calf, changed direction, and rushed it—only to find Sweet Fur Amy rushing him. He turned and ran. She chased him a long distance before she returned to Kapu.

"Bear fun," her whisking tail said. Kapu wagged his tail. Chasing a grizzly bear away from his prey was the height of wolf sport.

The fun over, Kapu got serious. He picked out an animal, and they all pursued it until they were successful.

Before he ate, Kapu left the three wolf hunters at the kill and carried food back to Aaka. She had not eaten the day before the birth. Now she would be hungry. He pushed the food into the den with his nose, and Aaka snatched it into the darkness.

Putting his head on his paws, holding his ears erect, he heard Aaka eat. Then he stretched out on his side and listened to the pups suckling. Every so often his tail wagged furiously.

Suddenly he sat up. A helicopter was hovering out on the tundra. He listened to it circle what he knew was the kill and his hunters. He waited, fearful it would swing over the den, but it did not. It rose high, circled the den area, then headed back toward the ocean.

It was midnight when Kapu returned to the kill finally to eat.

In ten days the puppies' eyes opened and they saw light at the end of the den tunnel. A few days later their ears opened and let in the sounds of their mother and their squirming siblings. No sooner could they see and hear than they began to growl, jump on each other, and fight.

On the day of the summer solstice, when the sun was as high as it would climb at noon and as high as it would be at midnight, the Avalik pups tumbled out of the den onto their Arctic playground. Seven fine pups bounced and growled.

The pack gathered to look them over. They noted Grappler's large body and head—a potential leader. They noted Smiler's friendliness. They approved of Black Lips's alert movements and of Long Face's steadiness, and they liked the two smallest ones, White Toes and Cotton Grass. They were sweet-tempered. They saw no outstanding features on the seventh pup, so she got neither a visual nor a scent name. She would have to go about her life and earn a name for herself.

When the adult wolves had sniffed, measured, and approved of each pup, Aaka led them back into the den—all but Grappler. He stayed outside to dig a hole. Sweet Fur Amy did not approve of this. Pups must obey the alpha female. She picked him up by the scruff of the neck and put him down in the den entrance. Aaka disciplined him with a growl-bark and herded him underground.

This was the debut of the wolf pups, their coming-out party. Each adult wolf had looked them over and noted their personalities. Some were strong, some were pleasant, some were quiet, but all were wonderful.

The debut was also the signal that the pups were being weaned. Solid food was needed.

Ceremony over, Kapu broke into the hunt howl, then ran off toward the Upper Colville River. He and his pack had culled out the weak and sick caribou near the den, and the ones that remained were too swift to catch. It was time to hunt farther afield in accordance with the plan of the wolf and the caribou.

Zing, Sweet Fur Amy, and Storm Call followed their alpha. They left the coming-out party and sped across green grass and blue moss. Lichen and Raw Bones trailed behind.

Uqaq did not go. Aaka had signaled her to stay with the pups. When she was nicely settled with them, Aaka took off. She leaped up the embankment to the tundra and ran like a winged creature until she was out of sight of the den. She was free. The pups no longer needed her every minute, day and night. Ears up, nose taking in the wonderful scents of blueberries and rabbit trails, Aaka exercised her leg and back muscles. She stretched her neck, shook her fur, and ran ten miles before turning back to Uqaq and her puppies.

The hunters did not turn back. They trotted at a constant, steady pace for one sunny day and one sunny night. This brought them to their Upper Colville River border. Kapu howled to tell the Mountain Pack they had arrived. Two strange wolves answered. Kapu howled again, then cocked his head to listen for Snow Driver and Cloud Berry. They did not answer. Nor did Ice Blink.

Kapu sniffed the air, whimpered his worried note, and scent marked the border. He walked away, came back, and scent marked again. Zing observed the crick of concern in Kapu's tail and stuck out his tongue to taste the scents on the air. A disturbing odor alerted him. Ice Blink had carried it, and Kapu had once kept her from joining the pack because of it. Worried, Zing too cricked his tail and marked the border.

Nervous about the change of power across the river, the Avaliks spread out and jogged along their border, marking it generously.

At midnight Kapu was about to go north when he heard snarling in the no-wolf zone. Up the embankment, out of the little willow forest, and over the Avalik border came a wild-eyed wolf drooling and panting.

Kapu waited for the Avalik border to stop him. It did not. The wolf came on. Kapu growled, "Stay where you are." The mad wolf did not. Kapu rose to his full height and roared out an avalanche of exploding growls. He flashed the white fangs under his black lips, stating his great power. He postured, "I am the alpha—obey."

The disease was driving the Mountain Pack wolf to do the unforgivable—attack an alpha. But the wolf who loomed before him was the most powerful wolf he had ever seen. His voice was deeper than the rumble of a glacial avalanche. He appeared to be as big as a grizzly bear. Thousands of years of wolf law held the mad wolf back. He cringed in agony before this thunderous alpha.

Kapu relaxed when he saw the wolf lower himself. That was a mistake. The wolf lunged. Kapu postured more strenuously. His fur rose higher, his teeth glistened more threateningly, his eyes narrowed, and once more he kept the rabid animal from biting him. Moments passed, then many minutes. Kapu trembled from exhaustion but held his advantage.

Suddenly a seizure shook the Mountain Pack wolf, and tortured for water he needed but could not drink, he charged once more. Kapu reared and the grasses trembled as he rumbled, "Stay."

Paralysis struck the rabid wolf to the ground; he yelped but could not move at all.

Kapu held his posture until life drained from the Mountain Pack wolf, then walked quickly away. Wolf society had defeated the disease. A strong leader was mightier than the virus.

Kapu returned to his pack but did not rest. A caribou was swimming frantically to his side of the river, headed right for the Avaliks. He puzzled over this for no more than an instant. A helicopter was circling the far side of the Colville, and Kapu recognized it. Its engine sound matched exactly the one he had heard before the dart had hit him. He started off for the den. Already his pack members were ahead, running as fast as they could toward home. They too recognized the copter.

The copter came on, then swerved, speeded up, and followed the Avaliks.

"There he is—that big black one. He's the alpha male."

"I'll run him down."

Kapu saw the copter coming toward him. He ran, ears back, tail down. The machine came on. He zigged. The copter zigged. He was being pursued. With the details of his territory vividly in mind, he turned completely around. He ran. It took the copter several minutes to maneuver a turn. Kapu noted that. When the thunder beater was almost overhead, he turned again. While the copter swung in a wide arc, Kapu headed for the fog rising off a sun-warmed pond. He trotted into the mist.

"Did you see where he went?"

"No. Lost him when we turned. He was running north when I last saw him, probably headed for the den."

"Where is it?"

"I don't know. I tried to get it out of Julie, but she wouldn't talk."

"Of course not."

The copter circled the rugged foothills, with their swales and threads of mist, then disappeared to the north.

Hours later Kapu caught up with his pack, who were milling in confusion during his absence. He tossed his head, and they quickly organized themselves and ran on.

Not far from the Avalik River, the wolves came upon a grizzly kill and shared his bounty in accordance with the laws of the wilderness. The bear would share their kills. The Avaliks were not bashful—each swallowed a huge amount of the food. There were seven pups to be fed.

As the wolves came to the top of the embankment, the pups saw, smelled, and heard the family. They pranced up to greet the adults and bounced, jumped up and down, and ran in circles. They followed the pack to the playground, running in and out between their legs.

The pup Long Face kept sniffing the air. Wonderful, mouthwatering food was somewhere in the midst of the adults, but where? Although he had never eaten meat before, he had seen his mother gobble it. He followed a meat trail to Kapu's mouth. He whimpered. Kapu turned his head away. Long Face stuck his nose in the corner of the mouth, where the food smelled strongest, and with that he signaled Kapu to feed him. Kapu regurgitated the food and put it on the ground. Long Face did not dally. He took a chunk in his mouth and swallowed it whole. Two other pups saw what was happening and stuck their noses in other adults' mouths. They, too, were rewarded.

When Aaka and Uqaq saw the pups eating whole food, they ran to the bear kill and returned with belly treats. Aaka fed the pups willingly, but Uqaq was reluctant. She wanted the food for her puppy self and held her jaws tightly closed. Then Grappler poked the corner of her mouth very hard, and the button went off. Up came the food.

By the end of June the pups were running in a pack. A tight little knot of legs, ears, and tails went down the embankment, along the beach, and back up to the den. Occasionally Smiler bumped into Grappler and the big pup growled. Smiler gave him a little space but not too much. The need for space had to be balanced with the need to move together. In mere days the pups achieved a perfectly coordinated puppy ballet—no one hitting another, all dashing, turning, and leaping to some inherited cue.

And then a strange thing happened. Despite Grappler's size and energy, the puppy pack began to follow Long Face. He was a pleasant pup who took up for the weaker ones. He defended little White Toes and Cotton Grass against the mob, and pushed Grappler away to let Black Lips eat. Leadership, the pups had discovered, is more than size and fearlessness. Compassion is what separates out the true leader, and so the pups followed caring Long Face.

The pups returned home one morning after digging a big hole. They collapsed on the playground, panting to cool off. Kapu was stretched out on his bed on the embankment top. He opened one eye and thumped his tail to greet them. Then a sound reached his ears and he was wide awake. He stood up. Quietly he walked down the embankment to the water's edge.

Willow Pup Julie came around the bend. She smiled and sat down on the beach some distance away. He lay down on his belly. They looked at each other. Finally she spoke.

"I've come to see your puppies, Kapu," she said. "It is that time of year." She put her chin in her hands, her elbows on her knees, and waited.

Kapu looked away. He knew why she was there, but he was not ready to honor her request. Right now

he did not want Willow Pup Julie to lay eyes on the most precious part of himself. Julie knew this. She picked up a stone and studied it.

"Peter Sugluk's group," she said in her soft voice, "won another dance prize. This one was Alaska's state prize, and he was the best of all the dancers."

Kapu heard the affection in her voice and relaxed. She talked on. "He won because he was you. He was magnificent just like you, and I missed you."

Kapu inched toward her. She sighed.

"Peter Sugluk and I still cannot get married." She tossed the stone. "He is going to school, and school is expensive." Kapu listened to the wistful longing in her voice.

"I will go to school, too. We need lots of money to live as husband and wife. I will study to be an animal biologist." She picked up another stone.

"Because of you I want to learn mammalogy. Dr. Hardy will teach me after school while I'm in high school. He is the science professor of the Iñupiat College in Barrow. So will Dr. Flossie Oomittuk, the veterinarian. They know a lot about animals, all right.

"I will live in Barrow with a schoolteacher friend of Ellen's, but I will come back to visit Amaroq and Nutik often. And I will look for you and call you." She was quiet while she thought for a minute.

"It seems strange to study animals in books—and in a town far away from them." Julie looked from the stone to Kapu's clear yellow orbs. He was looking directly at her. She noticed his rich black fur and how smoothly it lay on his muscular body. She noted his size and posture. He was half again bigger than she remembered. Alpha male wolves grow even after other members of their pack stop, and Kapu was no exception. Well aware of his stature, he held himself like the king he was.

"You have become a great leader like your father," she whispered. They both looked away and watched a leaf twisting in the wind.

After a while Kapu got to his feet. Julie got to her feet and walked quietly toward him. He waited for her. He was ready to take her to his pups. They climbed the embankment to the flower-edged playground.

"Kapu," she whispered, "they're wonderful. Ee-lie, Kapu, they're so cute." She dropped to all fours. The pups looked at her, then quickly at Kapu and Aaka. Their parents were not frightened. They looked at Uqaq, who was making a big fuss over Julie, her human mother. She even picked up a bone and gave Willow Pup Julie a toy.

"Good, Uqaq," Julie said and, pulling hard on the bone, played tug-of-war with her friend.

The pups looked from Uqaq to the other adults. They sent out no fear signals. Smiler sniffed Julie and edged closer. The seventh pup, now known as Nameless Moonlight, twisted her head to see better, and Grappler sat down. Long Face walked right up to her.

Julie bent over and sniffed him a wolf greeting. He sniffed her nose right back. One by one the others came up and greeted her. And each smelled the faint scent of Avalik about her. She was all right. Then Long Face wagged his tail and brought her a bone as a gift. She tucked it into her parka.

"Where's Amy?" she asked. Hearing her name, Sweet Fur Amy came to the top of the embankment with Storm Call.

"He's a fine one," Julie said, looking at the white puffs above the eyes of Storm Call and the dark-gray line down his nose. His cheeks and chest were like snow, his paws enormous.

"Where is Zing?" He too heard his name and stood up.

"And Silver? I don't see Silver." She did not appear. The wolves stared at Julie as if she should know.

For his part, Raw Bones hid in a blueberry patch.

Presently Julie got to her feet and walked down the embankment to the river shore. There she stopped and looked back.

Kapu was watching her from the top of the embankment. Raw Bones, feeling safe now that she was leaving, slunk to Kapu's side. Lichen squeezed in between the two and stared at Julie.

"Kapu," she said, "Aaka, Zing, Amy, Amy's friend, Uqaq, Raw Bones, his friend, and seven pups. My pack." She threw them a kiss and backed away.

"Silver is gone," she said to herself. "I am sad. Silver and I shared sorrow. We mourned together for Amaroq when he was killed. We nursed Kapu back to health when he was shot. I miss my beautiful friend."

She sang,

> "Silver, Silver, you are out on the tundra,
> Fly to the grasses,
> Fly to the lemmings,
> Fly to the foxes and owls,
> Fly to the grizzly,
> Fly to the caribou,
> And then you'll come back to your grandpups.
> That is how it is.
> Fly to your beautiful grandpups."

The wolves listened until a shifting wind carried her voice toward the ocean and she was out of sight.

With that they went back to their wolf work.

July is a busy time on the tundra. Baby birds flew, flowers bloomed, and young mammals bounced about. Butterflies flew to flowers and sipped their nectar. They held their wings at a tilt to catch the direct rays of the slanting Arctic sun and keep warm.

The pups were almost half grown. The time had come for wolf pup graduation.

On a bright day when the fuzzy fledglings of the water pipits were testing their wings, and the puppies were spilling out of the den to sleep in the doorway and on the playground, Aaka gave Kapu the signal: "It's time to go." By the rosy light of the midnight sun the Avalik pups graduated from the whelping den. They followed their pack northeastward.

Eventually they came to the summer rendezvous, an open tunnel on the top of a bluff above the Ikpikpuk River not far from the ocean. Down the slope lived an Arctic fox couple and their six bluish pups. A wolverine family denned in a swale nearby, and below the cliff on the gravel bars were nesting plovers, gulls, arctic terns, and jaegers. Multitudes of geese and ducks nested in the grasses at the edge of the river. Life had exploded in the sunny Arctic summer. The wolf pups watched everything that moved, played wolf pup jokes on unsuspecting tundra citizens, and stalked each other. They got into yipping and yowling fights, which Aaka and Kapu settled with sharp barks and nips.

One morning a helicopter flew overhead and the summer community disappeared from view. Jeremy Smith and Dr. Flossie Oomittuk were flying to Anaktuvuk Pass to inoculate the villagers' dogs against rabies. Jeremy spoke.

"Dr. Hardy still wants an alpha male wolf."

"I thought he had given that up," Dr. Flossie Oomittuk said, as if she hoped he had. Her tone ended the conversation. They looked down on the river and tundra. No wildlife was to be seen.

"I wish copters weren't so noisy," said the vet.

"Yeah, we miss a lot in this bus," said Jeremy. "But we also pick up a lot. We can pursue. I once wore down a wolf chasing him with this thing, and before he could catch his breath I darted him."

Flossie Oomittuk did not reply.

Nothing moved on the river clifftop until the helicopter had passed out of sight and sound. First a few birds went back to their young, then many. The foxes tiptoed out of hiding, and Long Face emerged from the open-ended tunnel. Not knowing about copters, he immediately led the pups on a tundra run. The nursemaid, Uqaq, cricked her tail and barked,

"Stay!" but the pups had no intention of obeying her. The day was bright, and wild things were flying and hopping everywhere. Uqaq barked again and again, but to no avail. When, at last, the pups disappeared into a swale, she picked up a bone in frustration and ran in circles with it.

Curiosity was driving the pups. No sooner had they chased a young weasel into its den than Long Face saw a gyrfalcon alight on the clifftop. He led an expedition to investigate it.

The stunning white falcon saw seven pups coming toward her and flew to her barely feathered nestlings. They sat on a ledge almost halfway down the high, steep cliff. Long Face looked down and saw them. He pursued, carefully manipulating the incline, his siblings behind. The falcon flew, climbed high above the pups, and folded her wings. She dove headfirst at the pack, strafing them with her talons and wings. Black Lips yelped and stumbled against Nameless Moonlight. Both lost their footing and plunged out of sight. The falcon struck again and Long Face took a blow on the shoulder. Instantly he came to his senses. He led a fast retreat.

When the pups had thundered back to the summer rendezvous, Black Lips and Nameless Moonlight were not with them. Aaka and Kapu immediately tracked the expedition back to the steep cliff. Far below on the rocks jaegers were screaming and feasting. The scent from their meal told of the tragedy. The parents howled in grief.

Kapu did not go back to the summer rendezvous. He signaled the pack and trotted inland. The clifftop was not healthy for pups who were not perfectly coordinated.

He stopped at a site that satisfied his wolf need to be the surveyor of the land. It was the top of a frost heave with a view in all directions. Aaka dug a pup bed behind a line of tundra grass tussocks. She did not dig a hideout tunnel, since the pups soon would be running with the pack.

The sun set in August, and the hours of darkness, though brief, chilled the air. A change set in. The caribou became restless. Birds took directional readings on the sun and pointed their beaks south. The Avalik pups were wiser but still impetuous.

Aaka kept a sharp eye on them. One evening she stared out across the tundra. The pups followed her gaze. There walked a grizzly bear. The pups were thrilled. Aaka read on. The bear's body language told her she had a cub. The pups could not read such tundra messages yet, and they tore off to see her. Aaka gave the alarm bark. Cotton Grass stopped.

Long Face, Grappler, Smiler, and White Toes did not. They ignored her warning and enthusiastically raced to the bear.

As they neared, a cub came out of a berry patch and bounced to his mother, who was glaring at the wolf pups. She let them come rollicking up, yipping and sniffing. When they were very close, she swung her huge paw. Smiler went flying into the air, then White Toes. She missed Grappler with the next blow and charged.

Suddenly fangs were set into her leg as Kapu took hold. At her armpit was Aaka. Zing and Storm Call danced before her while Raw Bones and Sweet Fur Amy dashed between her and the pups herding them back to safety.

Enraged by the pain, the two-ton grizzly rose to her hind feet. She swung her huge paws. The wolves let go, hit the ground, and dashed at her. She backed up, saying, "I surrender."

The bear snarled, her mouth wide open. The wolves flashed their teeth and breathed nasal threats, and the conflict ended. The grizzly turned and ran off with her cub.

The Avaliks whimpered and circled their dead pups, howling so long and pitifully that it seemed their hearts would break. But life went on. Kapu and

Aaka gently led Long Face, Grappler, and Cotton Grass back to the rendezvous.

Kapu lay down and crossed his forepaws. The wilderness was testing his pups. Four had lost the battle for wolf survival. "That is how it is," the Eskimos say, and in his way, so did Kapu. He lifted his eyes and focused on the living. Geese were flocking, and the ducks were back from the inland ponds with their new wing feathers. Ice crystals tickled his nose. He arose, and howling his deep minor note, he slid up an octave and held it there. The pack harmonized with him. It was time to take up the wandering life of the wolf.

The Avaliks jogged west looking over the caribou herds that were slowly moving south. Their rutting season was nearing and the bulls were collecting harems as they moved toward the forests. They held their big antlers high to display their power. In October they would not even eat, so intense would be their battles for mates. Now they were chasing each other in short spurts. Kapu took advantage of their preoccupation.

He split up a milling herd and isolated an old bull, who had a deep head wound from a rival's antler. He isolated a female with infected legs. He chased several calves and noted their good health. Three of his pups were alive and needed to be fed.

Kapu busied himself and the pack taking inventory of their herd. Winter was coming. The wolves took off.

As they ran, Kapu memorized the whereabouts of the ground squirrels, lemmings, hares, grizzly bears, moose, mice, and weasels. He noted the mosses and grasses that would soon be covered with snow. To these the caribou would come in winter. He noted the storm clouds and winds. All this knowledge became part of him.

Kapu and his pack were the stewards of their part of the Arctic tundra and as good stewards checked on its productivity.

In wind and ice storms and aching cold they traveled. Behind Kapu ran Zing, then Aaka and Lichen. Sweet Fur Amy trotted a little to Kapu's side, tasting the air for distant scents. Storm Call jogged in her shadow, followed by Uqaq. Tagging behind, listening and learning, came Long Face and Grappler. Raw Bones and Cotton Grass trod off to one side as the pack worked its way to the Nuka border.

Kapu stopped them at the no-wolf zone. He listened. A wolf had called to him. By his voice he knew he was not a Nuka. He was a traveler from the mountains. The lone wolf called again, his voice as melodic as a winter storm. To Kapu he was Wind Voice, a two-year-old. His birth pack was beyond the Mountain

Pack. He had traveled three hundred miles looking for a home. He was big, alert, and calm. Kapu read all this and invited him across the border for pack approval. Such a fine specimen should not be left for the Nukas. The Avaliks invited him into the pack. Wind Voice rubbed his scent into their ambrosia and proudly galloped off with his new family.

Twelve spirited Avaliks arrived outside Kangik on a cold September day. Men were packing sleds for the hunting season; their dogs were barking. A wet snow was being driven before a wind that was breaking the new ice on the Avalik River into chunky froth. The pack rubbed cheeks and bodies, exchanged scents, and howled.

Sweet Fur Amy broke away and loped to her viewing knoll. Her nose separated the multitude of scents. She identified dogs, whale meat, fish, people, oil, but not Nutik. She moved closer to the green house. A careful scenting told her Nutik was not there, nor were Julie, Kapugen, Ellen, or Amaroq.

She returned to the pack and through her lack of enthusiasm relayed the news. The green house was empty. Kapu led them away.

Running effortlessly through the snow, the Avaliks traversed their territory. They ran over frozen ponds and stopped to investigate snow machine tracks and snowshoe hare burrows. Eventually they wound up at their western border again.

Kapu had not tallied the Nukas when he was last here. He initiated a howl. The Avalik music had grown from an ensemble to an orchestra. Kapu's voice had deepened with his strengthening role, and Amy's clear voice had brightened. Aaka's howl was warmer and more melodious. Wind Voice added a rising portamento to the chorus. Everyone sang out in rich tones that spoke of the contentment and security of this well-ruled pack.

The Nukas answered. The alpha female, Moon Seeker, harmonized with a new mate. Low Wind was missing. Only five wolves answered, not nine.

Storm Call asked his relatives for the roster again.

Moon Seeker led off. By the end of the howl, Storm Call recognized only his mother and one brother. The others were wolves who had been invited into the pack. There was no shortage of food. Some tragedy had befallen the Nukas. Had the curse of Ice Blink traveled to this pack?

Kapu briefly scent marked the borders, scratched messages of no-trespass on the ground, and headed out for the Upper Colville River, where they howled to the Mountain Pack.

Their message went unanswered. The only sounds

were the distant bellows and roars of the caribou in the taiga. The rut was in full swing.

The Avaliks would not be challenged if they went over the border, but Kapu did not cross. He stopped at the no-wolf zone and rested his pack in the snow. Each groomed his or her fur with tongue and paws, and freshened ruffs with a roll in the snow.

Raw Bones grew restless. His home was a jog away. He yearned to return to it. As he started off, Kapu stopped him with a growl. The mad wolf was still in his mind. He led his pack away from the river.

The Avaliks wandered on, camping in old sleeping sites established by Silver and Amaroq and Amaroq's parents before them. At one site Uqaq found a bone toy and teased Cotton Grass with it until she broke down and played tug-of-war with her. Uqaq still loved being a puppy.

An early blizzard screamed in from the Arctic Ocean. Well fed and lazy, the Avaliks curled up near the Upper Colville. Noses buried in their tails, they watched the land and sky turn white.

Raw Bones got up, shook, and called to the Mountain Pack. The others listened for an answer, their eyebrows twitching under piles of snow. There was no reply.

After the storm ended, and hearing no voices in Raw Bones's old territory, Kapu decided to take it over. He led the Avaliks across their border, through the no-wolf zone, into the land of the Mountain Pack that had once belonged to Raw Bones. Each Avalik checked for wolves.

Raw Bones sped off to his den. Only a wolverine was there. Kapu went up the mountain. No wolves. Zing and Lichen checked along the river. They found only moose. Aaka, Amy, and Uqaq trotted over the low hills, and Storm Call and Wind Voice investigated the alders on the shore. Long Face took Cotton Grass and Grappler on a circular sniffing expedition. No wolves. The Avaliks were puzzled but eagerly enlarged their territory. Only Kapu and Sweet Fur Amy knew what had happened to the Mountain Pack. A faint stench of the rabies virus clung to the ground around their summer rendezvous.

Finding no alpha wolf to fight, Raw Bones ran his old trails. As he raced along the river and into the forest, his sense of power returned. He came down from his den that night and charged Kapu. Thoroughly bored by the ever-striving Raw Bones, Kapu simply stood up and loomed above him. He was once again bigger than Raw Bones. Obediently the would-be usurper gave up.

They traveled foothills, climbed mountains, and crossed creeks that drained out of the Brooks Mountains and never met another wolf.

When the Arctic night came to northern Alaska, the Avalik Pack were keepers of an enormous territory and Kapu was their wise and benevolent leader. He cared for them, watched over them, and led them to wholeness.

In late January Kapu walked to a knoll and looked down on the Ikpikpuk River. He was back on his father's original land. The breeding season was approaching—new pups—new enthusiasms. He lifted his head to sing when a helicopter clattered into the soundscape. He listened, ready to run, but the copter did not seek him out. It flew up the river and landed on the frozen Ikpikpuk, and he heard it no more.

The sky grew brighter. A glowing arc of yellow burned the eastern sky. Throwing back his head, Kapu called his pack to assemble. As they gathered around him, an orange fireball rose over the horizon. The sun was up again. A new year was beginning. The Avaliks pointed their noses to the sun and sang. They sang for many minutes, flooding the tundra with the most beautiful of all wilderness music—the call of the wolf to the new sun. Kapu sang a last note: "Let's run." Springing off his back feet, he vaulted down the knoll.

Fur rippling, the pack spent the next several hours running old family trails and sprinting after swift young caribou. When the caribou were out of sight, they trotted westward and looked at the musk oxen. In good spirits they circled back to the Ikpikpuk on their frozen river trail.

Suddenly Kapu buckled in the air and fell. He made no sound.

His foot was caught in a trap. He looked at the iron lock on his paw, got up, ran, and flipped in the air at the end of the chain. He lay still. The pack gathered around him staring at their helpless leader. They sniffed the trap, the chain, and the human scent that lay on the overturned snow. Aaka whimpered. Sweet Fur Amy bit the chain. Raw Bones dug at the base of the stake to which the chain was fastened. Storm Call and Wind Voice watched for the enemy. The loving wolves were in numb distress.

A snow machine roared in the distance, grew closer, and suddenly shot around the bend in the river. The wolves vanished into the low brush on the riverside. With a sled in tow two men climbed out of the machine and stopped short of the growling Kapu.

"What luck," said the Eskimo trapper, Benjamin

Ooglik. "He's in fine shape. Only been in the trap a few minutes. Pure black, too. He will make a fine parka ruff."

"No ruff out of this one," said Jeremy Smith forcibly. "He's the alpha male wolf of the Avalik Pack. My good friend Dr. Hardy wants him alive."

"Alive? Why is that?"

"For a medical study," answered Jeremy. Stepping back from Kapu, he shot a tranquilizing dart into his thigh. Kapu twitched but did not utter a sound. He clawed the snow until the drug took effect and he slumped into sleep. Jeremy opened the trap and examined the huge paw.

"Good trap. He's not even bruised."

"I told you so," said Ooglik. "Foam padding is good, all right."

They wrapped Kapu in a cargo net, tied him to the sled, and drove back to the copter near Benjamin Ooglik's house.

As soundless as falling snow, the wolves floated out of the brush and stood above the empty trap site.

The Avaliks had lost their great leader. Tragedy had called their name.

PART III

SWEET FUR AMY, THE NEW ALPHA

*T*he sun stayed up less than an hour that first day of its return—the day that Kapu vanished. When it set, the afterglow colored the white snowscape rose, violet, and then sea blue. The wolves milled shadowless around the cold spot where their leader had been.

They waited. He was not dead. There was no blood scent to say he had been killed. There were no tracks to say he had run away. He would be back. They called to him and waited for an answer. None came. They howled once more.

An Eskimo and his son, snowshoeing home after checking their trap line, heard the heartbreaking lost-alpha call of the wolves. Not knowing its meaning, they smiled.

"Good sound," said Akvik, the father. "The wolves are like us. They hunt in families. We are cousins." The Avaliks howled again.

"The tundra is all right," said his son, Nagiak. "The wolves are here. They take the sick and leave us the well." They hauled on their trapping sled and strode into the darkness.

The Avaliks called, off and on, until the sun came up at noon the next day; then they were silent. Each looked at the others waiting for someone to do something. They knew they must move on, but no wolf had the power to lead them. Kapu was gone. The pack was totally disabled.

It was Zing who finally acted. He went out on the frozen river to find Kapu. Lichen, Aaka, and Grappler followed.

That sparked Sweet Fur Amy to search up the mountainside with Storm Call and Uqaq. Raw Bones, seeing the pack break up, headed out for the Colville River. Eventually they all returned to the vanishing spot, even Raw Bones. There they waited. When a wolf leader is lost, the pack is lost. They broke up into smaller teams and hunted the moose and caribou that were bogged down in the snow.

After three weeks, Aaka felt a need to return to her den. Zing, Lichen, and Long Face followed the female alpha of the Avaliks. Sweet Fur Amy, Storm Call, Wind Voice, and Uqaq went up the river. Raw Bones, Grappler, and Cotton Grass took off for the foothills. The pack splintered into small pieces without their leader.

Before the Raw Bones team left the valley, another trap snapped and Grappler was caught. Cotton Grass lay down on her belly near her brother while Raw Bones stood back barking, ordering her to follow him. When she did not obey, he walked slowly back to join her and the struggling Grappler.

A snow machine buzzed in the distance. Raw Bones turned and sped away in terror. Cotton Grass caught his fear fever and ran after him. Far away from Grappler and the machine they slowed down and looked at each other. Even young Cotton Grass knew what the trap meant. Another Avalik was dead. Raw Bones whimpered. The pack that had been supporting him had fallen apart. Its leader was gone. Raw Bones didn't want to be on his own another moment. He lifted his nose and howled, "I'm here, where are you?" Cotton Grass joined him. From far away Aaka, Lichen, Long Face, and Zing answered. From another direction Sweet Fur Amy, Storm Call, Uqaq, and Wind Voice howled, "Here, here, here." The three groups called back and forth, trotted toward each other, howling until they met.

Ten Avaliks licked cheeks on a wind-packed land rise between the den and Kangik. They wagged tails and whimpered. Cotton Grass's pained cry told them another pup had failed the hard test of a wolf's first year of life. They sang for Grappler, milled around, ran off in their splinter groups, and came back together.

Without Kapu they were lost. Raw Bones at last saw his opportunity to become alpha.

Sweet Fur Amy smelled prey and signaled her group to follow her. She jogged off on the scent of a lone caribou. Raw Bones eagerly joined her. Cotton Grass, Aaka, and Zing came along.

Three miles along, when the prey was in sight, Sweet Fur Amy sent her hunters to the right and left of it. The animal was in a wind-cleared area where a caribou could run well. She and Kapu usually drove prey toward deep snow to slow it down. She signaled Raw Bones to her side. He ignored her. He would lead. He ran full out for the caribou. It turned back to the hard-packed meadow, quickly got up speed, and outran Raw Bones and the pack.

Sweet Fur Amy trotted on. When she scented an old cow, she took the lead again. Aaka and Zing came with her. Snarling Raw Bones ran into first place. To Raw Bones females were the alphas of the pups and of social interactions and, in Sweet Fur's case, of finding the game—but she was not and would never be the alpha of the kill. He ran ahead of her. She swept ahead of him. He nudged her off the trail. She snapped at him. Zing, trotting in second place, watched passively. He was content with his role as vice president. He had held this position for so many years, he could not change. Wind Voice ran with Zing.

When Raw Bones passed Sweet Fur Amy again, the caribou saw him and fled. Amy, by raising her head and tail above his, sent Raw Bones to the rear. Head down, tail lowered, he stayed there.

Two hours later they felled an arthritic bull, and Sweet Fur Amy ate first. She was not hesitant. She had been chosen by her father to lead the hunts, and now that he was gone, she was the leader of the Avaliks.

For six weeks they followed her, but loosely. The pack was made up of strong individuals, and they were still disorganized as they tried to make their own packs. But obedience to the leader was in their genes, and Sweet Fur Amy slowly brought the pack into harmony.

The month of March came, the only time of year that female wolves can breed. Sweet Fur Amy refused Storm Call's invitation. Pups would confine her to the den for two weeks, and her leadership was not secure enough for that. Without her the pack would fight and break apart. She needed every member.

Raw Bones, knowing pups were strength and ignoring wolf custom, approached submissive Uqaq. It is, however, the female who decides whose traits will be passed on to her pups. Uqaq snapped at Raw Bones and ran off with the handsome Wind Voice.

Pups!

Sixty-three days later the pups were due. Raw Bones took over. He wanted pups, any pups, to be born on his own territory. In a fierce battle he fought off youthful Wind Voice and, with coaxing and sweet whimpers, led Uqaq to the Colville River den. Sweet Fur Amy could not make Uqaq obey her and stay at the Avalik den. Raised in captivity, Uqaq had never learned the birthing laws of the wolves, and she followed her father. Wind Voice took his place behind them.

Sweet Fur Amy took the rest of her pack to the shabby den on the Upper Colville River. Her nieces and nephews must have a society to grow up in.

Raw Bones cleaned and reconstructed the battered den while Wind Voice watched in confusion, not understanding the strange rules of his new pack.

The next night nine pups were born. Excitement ran high. Pups! The Avaliks mingled, rubbed scents, licked cheeks. Pups! Their summer work was cut out for them.

Hearing them suckle inspired Sweet Fur Amy, and she organized her allies, Aaka, Zing, Lichen, and Storm Call, into a cooperative hunting team. She took them out each evening to harvest injured calves and ill cows and bring the food many miles to Uqaq. Wind Voice stayed at the den to protect his fatherhood rights from Raw Bones. They fought often.

When the pups were two weeks old, Uqaq became impatient with them. They nursed relentlessly. They fought each other. She could not keep them clean. She did not know how to discipline them. All she wanted to do was get away from them. When she could not take the yelping and suckling another minute, she ran out of the den and down to the river.

She stood with her tail between her legs. She did not know how to be a mother. Her puppyhood had been in human arms, her sustenance a bottle. She had no memory of Silver and how she had cleaned and nursed her. She had been too weak to do anything but whimper and sleep.

Wind Voice barked, telling her to return, but she had never truly bonded with him. She had no knowledge of a father's importance either. She looked at the other side of the river and waded in.

Aaka and Sweet Fur Amy rushed to her. She walked deeper and, catching sight of Raw Bones on the other side of the river, she swam across to him, whimpering and woofing. Even Raw Bones did not know what to do with a mother who deserted her pups. He had not counted on that. He turned and ran. Then Uqaq ran.

Sweet Fur Amy and Aaka watched the strange behavior, then walked through the alders and back to the den. They had a job to do.

The hungry pups waddled out of the nursery whimpering and crying piteously, searching for their mother and milk. They leaped up at Sweet Fur Amy's belly to nurse. They knocked Aaka down and crawled over her. Feeling puppy feet and suckling mouths, her maternal instincts surged through her. She lay as still as she had with her own pups. They suckled her voraciously. Had they nursed her empty teats long enough—several days—she would have produced milk. But Uqaq returned, and the pups abandoned milkless Aaka and swarmed over their mother. Uqaq rolled her eyes, let them nurse a few minutes, then broke away. She swam across the river again.

The pups followed her, sniffed the river, got water up their noses, and yelped in pain. Sweet Fur Amy and Aaka picked them up by the scruffs of their necks and carried them to the den entrance.

Aaka did not have time to let the pups stimulate her mammary glands, and when they had fallen asleep from exhaustion, she and Sweet Fur Amy signaled Storm Call. Messages went from wolf to wolf. Long Face trotted off to find Uqaq; Aaka and Cotton Grass stayed with the pups. Raw Bones sat on a knoll defending his property, and Sweet Fur Amy, Lichen, Storm Call, and Zing went north. Wind Voice kept his eye on Raw Bones.

Sweet Fur Amy and her group traveled in constant sunlight and did not stop until they were on the rise above the green house. Leaving Storm Call and Lichen behind, Amy ran down the incline to Julie's door. Julie was not there. Amy trotted on through the town, passing people who were packing sleds for fish camp. Quick sniffs told her Willow Pup was not among them. She ran up the slope to the Quonset hut. The dogs were gone. Nutik had been tied there, she noted, but he, too, was missing. The sled was gone.

The schoolhouse door was ajar. Sweet Fur Amy looked in and focused her yellow eyes. Amaroq and Ellen were inside. She called to the boy, "I'm your friend," and he stopped scribbling on the blackboard and ran to the front step.

"Come here," he howl-barked happily to Sweet

Fur Amy. She stepped forward, and Amaroq wolf-whimpered a pleasant greeting. Sweet Fur Amy lowered her tail in disappointment. The scent of Willow Pup Julie was faint on the boy. She had not been here for a long time. With a woof-bark she greeted him, then sped like a jaeger's shadow over the tundra to Storm Call and Lichen. Her body language said, "Back to the Colville."

Sweet Fur Amy was on her own. Willow Pup Julie could not help these pups as she had their mother, Uqaq, and Uqaq's brother, Nutik.

Along the route home the wolves stopped at an old frozen kill and packed their stomachs with good food.

They crossed the river, threaded through the dwarf alders, and approached the den.

Growling ferociously, Raw Bones rushed at Sweet Fur Amy. She ignored him—an insult that dropped him to his belly. He groveled to her. Every wolf saw his shame.

Sweet Fur Amy walked to the pups, who were now too weak to suckle. She stood above them waiting to be asked for food with a poke in the corner of her mouth. They were not able to give this signal. They knew only how to nurse. Their pitiful voices weakened.

Sweet Fur Amy leaned down to the pup Big Ears and opened her mouth to let the scent of food pour out. He sniffed and tried to suckle her lips. That misplaced touch did it. Sweet Fur Amy delivered food.

Big Ears licked it, then gulped chunks whole. Owl Feathers, named for the white tufts of puppy fur behind her ears, caught on and touched Storm Call's mouth. Bird Egg, with the rounded head, begged from Lichen. The others were too weak to learn. They whimpered and fell asleep. The three wolves trotted back for more food. This time Wind Voice went with them. Raw Bones was still humbled by Sweet Fur's insult.

Three pups survived: Big Ears, Owl Feathers, and Bird Egg.

One misty day Sweet Fur Amy was coming home through the dwarf alders with pup food when Raw Bones jumped out and grabbed her throat. She angrily twisted him over her back. He let go.

Sweet Fur Amy had had enough of Raw Bones. She fought with her teeth, a rare event among wolves, and he went down for a last time.

Totally humiliated, Raw Bones slunk away. Even his fur clumped in gobs, reflecting his mood. Sweet Fur Amy watched him cross the Colville carrying his tail not only between his legs but up against his belly. He would not be back.

Uqaq, who was still hiding out on the other side of the river, ran to him and begged him to let her join him. He ignored her. He was too low in spirits even to give her an invitation. He had been defeated before, but never on his own territory. To be subdued at his den site was more than defeat. It was living death. No spurt of energy, no fire of purpose could change it.

Uqaq sensed all this and turned back. Raw Bones could not help her.

In late July Sweet Fur Amy moved the pack and the three pups to the Avalik summer rendezvous. Along the way they came upon Raw Bones feeding at one of their old kills. His fur was rumpled and unkempt. His tail was pressed up under his belly. The pack did not run him off the food. Although he was defeated, he was part of the tundra community—the lone wolf surviving on old carcasses and the small mammals the wolves so carefully cultivated. Sweet Fur Amy nosed Owl Feathers, Bird Egg, and Big Ears on down the trail to the bluff above the Ikpikpuk River. The eight older wolves followed them.

One day the copter flew overhead carrying the vet and the pilot to the Eskimo villages to inoculate dogs. The Avaliks lowered their tails and lay down.

"There's Julie's wolf pack," Jeremy Smith said. "You know, I finally got the alpha for Dr. Hardy."

"I know," she said coolly.

"He's finished his research," pilot Smith went on. "The alpha heart rate is normal and steady when he's with a low-ranking member of his society. The omega's heart raced like a jackhammer in the presence of the alpha." Flossie Oomittuk did not comment.

"When he returned them to the captive pack," Jeremy went on, "it worked the other way. The alpha's heart rate went up with the pressure of all his responsibilities, the omega's down. We are learning the effects of leadership on social animals like us."

Flossie listened and stared at the river below.

"What are they going to do with the black alpha now that the experiment is over?" she asked.

"Send him to a zoo."

The helicopter clattered on toward Anaktuvuk Pass.

On the ground Sweet Fur Amy waited until the earshattering sound of the copter had faded, then checked her family. They were all there. No traps had gone off. She sat down and watched the terns and gulls circle over the river.

The days shortened. The permafrost, which had

thawed about eighteen inches during the summer, froze solid again. Sweet Fur Amy felt the messages from the sun and the ground and led her pack off the bluff and out onto the tundra. Owl Feathers, Bird Egg, and Big Ears could have benefited from more pouncing and stalking lessons, but they were wiry and strong like Wind Voice, their father. It was time to teach them how to hunt and to help them learn to avoid the perils of winter. They were full grown but not hunters. They knew nothing about the death blows of caribou and moose; they did not know how to attack or to work with an organized hunting group. It would take all winter to teach them.

That night the Avaliks loped along through falling snow, mouths slightly open in wolf smiles as they melted ice crystals on their tongues. The time of the gypsy wolf was here, and their spirits were high. They moved gracefully, occasionally bounding like dancers and stretching their long legs as far as they could. The land lay flat and silver-gray before them. Winter clouds with their blue-black bottoms scurried above them. Julie's wolves were free and running behind a trim and warmhearted female alpha.

Sweet Fur Amy rested the pups at daylight and urged them on at sundown.

When they reached the banks of the Meade River, Sweet Fur Amy made a longer stop at a sleeping site where Kapu liked to rendezvous. It was close to an overwintering caribou herd and only a night's trot from Kangik. They rescratched old beds, howled a song of wandering and winter, then lay down. The pups flopped without making beds and were instantly asleep. Their underfur had grown so dense with the shortening days that they were now wrapped in warm, thick blankets.

As the moon rose above a low bank of black clouds, the earth began to shake. Sweet Fur Amy awoke. She got to her feet. An enormous herd of caribou was clicking and snorting just over the horizon. Something was wrong. They were moving north when they should be moving south. She strained all her senses.

The hordes were boxing themselves into a land corner. Caribou are leaderless herds, not thinking packs. They had cropped the grasses and lichens in front of them eating their way north. Near the ocean they turned around but could not go south. There was no food in that direction. They had eaten and trampled it all. The trapped caribou were starving.

Hearing the distress in their bleats, Sweet Fur

Amy jumped on her hind feet and signaled the pack—even the pups—to come see what was happening. They raced north to the horizon, stopped, and looked. Sweet Fur Amy picked out a hungry cow and, with Storm Call's cooperation, split her off from the edge of the enormous herd. Using her own style, not Kapu's, she signaled Zing to the left.

Accustomed to Kapu, he misunderstood her and ran straight at the cow. Storm Call, who did understand Sweet Fur, tried to compensate for Zing's mistake. He came in from the left, cutting off Aaka. Confused, Aaka stopped. The cow sprinted away and was lost to scent and sight.

They selected another.

Two days later they still had not eaten. Aaka felt the need to try her skills. After rolling in the snow to clean her fur, then stretching and yawning, she howled the hunt song and sped toward the bleating herd. Zing followed her, happy to be beta to Kapu's female alpha. Long Face followed Zing. Uncle Zing was his role model. He imitated his movements, followed him everywhere, and now joyfully jogged behind him. Cotton Grass trotted behind her brother. To her Long Face was still the alpha pup to follow. He was a regal wolf with his rime-gray fur and dark facial mask, and she adored him. Long Face saw her tracking him and whisked his tail to tell her where to go. Alphaness was growing in him.

Sweet Fur Amy watched Aaka's group depart but did not join them. Her instincts told her she must go back to her first talent—finding the scent of a sick caribou and tracking it down. That was what her pack respected her for, and that was what would bring Aaka back to her. She rounded up Storm Call, Wind Voice, Uqaq, and Lichen and took off. She did not like the feel of having two groups, her mother's and hers. It was not good wolfdom.

On the edge of the big herd she picked up the odor of a young caribou with an advanced leg infection, and she and her hunters easily claimed her. Feeling like an alpha, Sweet Fur Amy howled to announce the feast to her whole pack. They were not long in joining her. Her mother's group stayed somewhat apart. After eating, they slept on separate frost heaves.

Sweet Fur Amy knew what must be done.

A few days later, when the food was eaten, she danced and threw up her head to get their attention, then led them on a run. She was going to circle their territory as her father had done when members were not cooperating. After two weeks they came back to the campsite licking cheeks and mixing scents. They scratched their beds close together. Once more the land had bonded them.

By December the boxed-in caribou were dying. They snorted and bleated in the darkness. When the sun came up in January, thousands were strewn across the tundra. The Avaliks inspected the disaster, but moved away when humans arrived in the area. In planes and helicopters, on snow machines and sleds, they came to study the phenomenon and to figure out what the wolves already knew. Sweet Fur Amy led her pack back to the Avalik River.

In March, when the vernal equinox divided the day into twelve hours of sun and twelve hours of no sun, Storm Call was Sweet Fur Amy's shoulder-to-shoulder companion. He did not just run beside her, he ran close, touching her cheeks, her ears, and her nose. She was coming into estrus, and he would be her mate. Cotton Grass was also coming into estrus. She too wanted this fine gray wolf. She flirted with him, whimpered love notes, and begged him to romp with her. Storm Call ignored her. He and Sweet Fur Amy had been loving friends since the day he had come over the Nuka border. That day they had chosen each other and could not be separated.

They mated when the herds of caribou that had

migrated to the forest in October were on their thundering march north.

Pups! The message shot through the Avaliks' scent system, inspiring whimpers, tail wags, and cheek licks. It also sparked a trip to houseclean the den above the Avalik River.

Sweet Fur Amy enthusiastically cleared out the debris of winter and dug the ancestral nursery doorway wider. The years of excavation had expanded the length of the passageway to almost four feet. After looking over the home, she took it upon herself to enlarge the whelping room. She stopped when she could lie on her side with her feet outstretched. The den was as cold as the permafrost, about eighteen degrees Fahrenheit, but Sweet Fur Amy did not feel the chill through her dense winter underfur, nor would the pups. She would snuggle them into her belly fur. Pups. At last, her own pups.

Sweet Fur crept out of the den, breathed a deep draft of air, and walked to the top of the embankment. The icy world sparkled in all directions around her, and as if to make it prettier, the wind lifted snow and carried it like a scarf over the river. Sweet Fur Amy was at peace. Pups. Storm Call came to her side. She licked his chin and cheek. He was the alpha male and would take her place for about ten days when she disappeared into the nursery to give birth and tend helpless infants.

Suddenly she cocked her head. The wind had changed. On it was information she had not picked up before. She licked far around her nose and muzzle to gather scents and confirm the news.

Without a sound she crossed the snowy tundra and trotted up a slight rise. A white-walled Eskimo hunting tent sat in a swale out of the wind. Heat radiated from it, and as she already knew, Willow Pup Julie and Peter Sugluk were inside. They were talking softly to a third Eskimo, the dancer Steven Itta. He had joined his friends to help them set up camp.

Peter put his arm around Julie. "How can this wonderful thing be happening to us?" he said.

"Ee-lie," she answered softly. "To think the college is paying us to live on the tundra."

"How did this come about?" asked Steven. "I haven't heard the whole story."

"It's a good story, all right," said Julie.

"It began," said Peter, "when Flossie Oomittuk learned Dr. Hardy was going to send Kapu to a zoo.

"She went right to his office and told him that science would be better served if Kapu was released on his territory.

"Then she said, 'You know what an alpha wolf's

heart rate does, but you don't know what happens when an alpha who has been long removed returns to his pack.'"

"'They'll kill him,' said Dr. Hardy.

"'We don't know that,' said Flossie Oomittuk, 'but I do know who could find out.'

"'Who?' he asked.

"'Julie Edwards, your afternoon student,' Dr. Oomittuk said. 'Her father is the famous elder Kapugen. He tells me she lived seven months with the wolves of the Avalik. Your black wolf is their alpha. She calls him Kapu. I took her to see him, and she cried. Then she talked to him in wolf talk. Kapu became very calm when she spoke.'

"'So?' Dr. Hardy asked her. 'What are you suggesting?' And Dr. Oomittuk reminded him that Jane Goodall had lived with wild chimpanzees in the African game preserve of Gombe. She learned all about them. She learned chimpanzees are quite like people—they are jealous, respectful, playful; they love and mourn—and much, much more.

"Then Flossie said, 'We have our own Jane Goodall. She is Julie Edwards. Her Eskimo name is Miyax. She is well known as Julie of the Wolves. She could live on the tundra as she has before and study the wolves.' He was quiet, so she went on talking.

"'We need to know more about wolf society. Wolves are very important. They are our brothers.'

"'You're right,' Dr. Hardy finally said. 'Bring her to my office and we can talk about it.'"

Julie listened to Peter as she pulled off her warm sealskin parka. Her thoughts went back to the day she had gone with Flossie Oomittuk to Dr. Hardy's office. She recalled how he looked out the window at the vast tundra and said, "Flossie wants you to have this job, but I would not go out there by myself. How can I be responsible for sending you?"

Without a moment's hesitation she had said, "Peter Sugluk and I wish to marry. The tundra is our home. Two are safer than one and two can do a better job than one." The professor's face had become thoughtful. Peter Sugluk was well known. He had won the Kivgiq Award. He had herded musk oxen for Kapugen, and he had come from Siberia, where he had lived with his family in the manner of his Eskimo ancestors.

Julie recalled Dr. Hardy folding his hands on his desk and telling her that under those conditions, she had the job. She could still feel her face glow and her heart beat hard as she realized she and Peter could get married and be paid to live as they wanted to live.

With a happy smile she stirred the caribou stew bubbling on the kerosene stove. Steven Itta was packing his sled bag to leave.

"One more question," he said. "My mother will want to know where you were married."

"In my father's house," said Julie. "In Kangik." Her words brought back memories of that day. She recalled the minister from Barrow in his black suit and white collar as he stood in front of the stack of furs. Peter was dressed in a reindeer shirt with an ermine ruff. She was wearing a white Eskimo dress trimmed with rich embroidery from Japan. Ellen and Kapugen wore their dress clothes. Their boots were elaborately decorated with black-and-white calfskin and laced with caribou hide. Amaroq wore the cowboy suit his Minnesota grandmother had sent him, and Nutik sported a beaded collar. A few close friends stood beside Kapugen and Ellen.

Outside, the villagers were waiting until the ceremony was over and Julie and Peter came out to greet them. Then tundra drums throbbed, voices rose in song, and Peter swept Julie up in his arms and kissed her lovingly. As she hugged him back, the villagers began to dance and cheer. Drums beat. He put her down, and breathlessly she slipped her arm around him. Together they greeted the wedding guests. Then the maktak and whale stew were served. The party lasted far into the night, she was told, for she and Peter slipped away early and went out to their tent on the tundra.

"I hope Kapu returns in good spirits," Steven said as he finished a bowl of stew before departing.

Sweet Fur Amy walked restlessly back to her pack.

She had heard the name Kapu.

Snow began falling.

The Avaliks, sparked into play by the swirling flakes, ran out onto the tundra. They pranced and rolled in the clean snow. Storm Call put his cheek and shoulder in it and pushed until he rolled on his back. When he was sweet-clean, he stood up. His tail whisked once, then twice. He could hear the *click-click* of the caribou coming north to their calving grounds. He howled. The pack howled; then, pushing off with a flying leap, their fur blowing and swinging, they trotted out to meet them.

The herd was miles long and miles wide. The Avaliks ran among them, judging them and herding them into little groups. Spring was upon the Arctic tundra.

When her pack had eaten, Sweet Fur Amy led

them off to check out the Nukas. At their border they howled. The Nukas answered. Sweet Fur absorbed their information: eight adults and three adolescents—and they were on Avalik land. They had slunk over the agreed border at the National Petroleum Reserve outpost. Sweet Fur Amy was too pregnant to lead a territorial fight, so she resorted to other wolf weapons. She scratched the ground and lifted her leg to border mark. Then she howled and started a voice contest. The two packs howled back and forth until Sweet Fur Amy conceded them the stolen land. She did not need it. Much of the western calving grounds were hers, as well as Raw Bones's old territory. The Nukas were pleased with the treaty. They howled friendly quips to their relatives Storm Call and Lichen.

Coming home, Sweet Fur Amy made a side trip to the rise that looked down on the green house. Voices murmured.

Ellen was reading aloud to Amaroq. Nutik was curled on the front step with his ears straight up listening to the tundra and the village.

Sweet Fur Amy called to him. He called back but did not move.

The CB crackled.

"Aapa, Daddy," said Julie.

"I hear you, Miyax. Over."

"Amy is very pregnant. The den is ready. The pups will soon be born. It is time to release Kapu. Over."

"Good. I shall get Dr. Hardy on the lab radio. Is Amy there now? Over."

"No, I heard her call from somewhere near you. She likes to talk to Nutik. Take him inside, and she will go home.

"Let me know when Dr. Hardy gets the cage out of Barrow onto the tundra and opens the door. Over."

"Roger. Over and out."

When the Willow Pup Julie voice stopped, Kapugen opened the house door. Amaroq ran out, put his arms around big, handsome Nutik, and led him inside. Sweet Fur Amy waited a short while. Finally she woof-barked and trotted back to the pack. They were waiting for her not far from Kangik.

Then in scent and sound she said, "Pups," and hurried to the den. They followed, kicking up little storms of snow in excitement. The entire pack ran right past Julie and Peter, who were stretched out on caribou skins not far from the den. They were mere residents of the tundra, like the wolverines and grizzly bears.

"Here they come," Julie whispered into a recorder. "Right to the den." Peter watched through binoculars.

"Amy's ears are back," Peter said. "She looks serious."

Julie recorded his words on tape as well as this: "Amy's mate is scanning the tundra. His hackles are up. He looks like he will take on the world to protect his pups."

"Zing is here with his pretty mate," Peter whispered, and pointed down the river.

"Here comes my dear friend Aaka," said Julie. "She is crossing the thawing river. Three pups are with her. They are well-trained adolescents and friendly. They wag their tails a lot and lick Aaka's cheeks.

"Now the handsome stranger we named Strong has joined Aaka and the pups. He is watching them anxiously as they cross the water and ice. They stick close to him and lick his cheeks. He must be their father.

"Alpha Pup, his sister, and now Uqaq are here. They all know that Amy's hour has come."

The tundra was quiet. Sweet Fur Amy paced the playground, avoiding stepping on the tiny sweetpeas that were blooming there. The others lay down, got up, dug beds, and watched her. Soft human voices reached their ears. They paid them no heed, even though the humans were walking upright. Peter went to work to kill time; Julie went into the tent.

"Aapa," Julie said into the CB, "has Kapu been released? Over."

"Well, funny thing, all right," he answered. "We're here inside Avalik territory, and the cage door is wide open, the humans are gone, but he won't leave. He hangs at the very back of the cage. Even food on the ground does not lure him out. Dr. Hardy is watching from a distance. Over."

"That's interesting, all right," said Julie. "I must think about that. Over. Out."

Julie did think about it while Peter Sugluk checked the caribou carcass that he had hung on a rack. He looked at the wolves, decided nothing was happening, and picked up his axe. He climbed down a ladder into the refrigerator he was digging. He worked for a while, then sought Julie.

"We've got to get our food underground," he said. "It's beginning to thaw."

"I don't have much to do until Kapu runs free," said Julie. "I will help you."

The morning passed. Peter Sugluk and Julie worked at the refrigerator. Then at noon Peter carried smoked meat from the tent to a five-by-ten-by-five-foot wooden box on a sled. It stood behind the tent. Inside the box were skins, a kerosene stove, and food containers. Two months from now, when it was cold, he and Julie would hitch this warm home to the snow machine and follow the wolves in winter.

Julie walked out on the embankment thinking about Kapu and watching Sweet Fur Amy.

She went into the tent in the early evening.

"Kapugen, do you hear me? Over."

"I hear you, Miyax," he answered. "Pups? Over."

"Pups soon. Amy is in the den. She has not come out. What about Kapu?"

"Kapu won't leave the cage. Over."

"I have thought of something. Over."

"What is it? Over."

"Remember how Nutik had his own little comfort space behind the water barrel? He would go there when strangers came into the house, and he would feel safe. Over."

"But he eventually came out," Kapugen said. "Kapu has not. Three days have passed. He needs food. Over."

"Cut a hole in the rear of the cage," Julie said. "Humans came in through the front door of the cage to feed him. The front is filled with bad dreams. Open his comfort space to the tundra. Over."

"All right," said Kapugen. "That is good wolf thinking. I'll tell Dr. Hardy. Over. Out."

Julie glanced at the wolf den. Storm Call was snoozing with his head on his crossed paws. Nothing was happening.

She climbed down into the refrigerator with Peter and chipped at the rocklike permafrost with her ulo. Together they made a little progress.

"How do the wolves dig in this?" Peter Sugluk asked, and climbed to the surface to dump a small bucket of the earth and gravel he had chipped away. Suddenly he backed down. "Miyax," he whispered. "The wolves are up. They are restless."

Julie climbed out of the refrigerator and crept toward the den on all fours.

Storm Call was standing at the entrance staring into the darkness. Owl Feathers and Bird Egg stood beside Aaka and Zing on the far side of the playground.

Julie lay still. Snowbirds were sitting on their eggs. Water pipits were circling their nests. Snowy owls were hunting lemmings. At three A.M. Julie spoke into the tape recorder.

"A pup has been born. The father is on his elbows

looking into the den. He is smiling and wagging his tail."

By eight o'clock in the morning six explosive wags of Storm Call's tail had announced six pups.

Pups! Sweet Fur Amy's pups. Owl Feathers lay close to the den entrance, ready to be a baby-sitter. Zing and Lichen ran in circles. Uqaq, Long Face, and Cotton Grass romped to the top of the embankment and chased each other, scratching up the last patches of snow.

The crackling CB brought Julie back to the tent.

"Miyax, do you read me?" Kapugen asked. "I'm back at the Arctic Research Lab in Barrow. Over."

"I hear you, all right, Aapa," Julie said, then quickly added, "Six pups have been born. Over."

"That is good news, all right," said Kapugen. "And I have good news. Your thoughts were right. Dr. Hardy and I cut off the back of the cage. Before we reached the truck, Kapu walked out of the cage and devoured the food we had left for him. Over."

"That is very good. I am so very happy. Kapu is free. Over."

"He was calm," said Kapugen. "He ate the whole meal, then looked about. He seemed to know where he was. Then he walked away. Over."

"He was calm, you say? Over."

"It was as if nearly a year in a laboratory had never happened. He walked, then trotted. His radio collar says he is going right straight for the Avalik River den. He's yours now. Over. Out."

"Kapu," Julie whispered. "Kapu's coming home." Her eyes glistened with unspilled tears.

She sat on her caribou skin, feet out straight.

"Now what will happen?" she asked herself, and watched a silvery fog roll in.

Out of scent range of the men, Kapu rolled in the snow, cleaned his fur, and groomed his tail with his teeth. The fog rolled over him. He closed his yellow eyes, sniffed deeply, and read the information held in the moist fog droplets.

The caribou were far south. Arctic foxes were scarce. Lemmings were scarce. Plant life was scarce, eaten and trampled by the caribou mistake. He lifted his head high. His yellow eyes brightened. A more important message was in the droplets. The Nukas were on Avalik territory. The fur rose on his back. He took off for the border, where he discovered from the scent marking that a new border had been established by the Avaliks and Nukas on Avalik property. He was irked until he came upon the truly important message: Sweet Fur Amy was the alpha of his pack—

and pregnant. Pups! He lifted his leg high and scent marked.

Avoiding Kangik, he set off for the den on the Avalik River. Around ten o'clock the fog burned away, revealing a tundra flashing with wildflowers and small birds on wing. He stopped and took in the scene before him. Under blue-gray clouds in bright sunlight lay an endless tundra with its cycling future. It erased the memory of men poking him, and voices, radios, and other annoying equipment that had been attached to his body. Before him caribou were giving birth, wolf packs were cuddled around puppy-filled dens, and he could run forever.

He shook his head and was reminded of the radio collar around his neck. It rested comfortably. He ignored it, breathed deeply, and walked on.

Then he heard Storm Call leading a hunt.

He did not go to the den. The Avaliks were stable under Sweet Fur Amy's leadership and Storm Call's intelligence. He turned around and went back to the Nuka border.

With great gulps he dined on one of their recent kills, then trotted into their territory and lifted his leg high, higher than ever before. He sprayed again and again as he pushed his western border back into Nuka land.

He whisked his tail at them and walked slowly back to the kill. He had played a wolf joke on the Nukas. His scent marks had put the kill on his side of the border. The Nukas would not be able to reach their food. He howled to them, but they did not answer. They had withdrawn to their den.

Kapu was back.

He trotted on south into the foothills and to the edge of the Colville River valley. The embankment where he had so often established borders was not marked. The no-wolf zone was gone. Kapu went down the slope, wound among the alders, and surprised a moose and her calf. She charged him. He turned and chased her, separating the two. She did not run far but stopped, turned around, and stood belly deep in the little trees ready to kill for her calf.

Kapu sent her the "not interested" message, jogged to the river, and crossed it. He wandered the empty home of the Mountain Pack for several days. He took down an old arthritic caribou bull and dined. Well stuffed, he visited the den Raw Bones had so persistently coveted. Uqaq had given birth here, he read.

He trotted back to the Colville River and plunged into it. He swam to a deep pool and paddled in circles until he had washed off the disinfectants, shots, and other human odors embedded in his thick underfur.

"Dr. Hardy to Julie. Do you hear me? Over."

"I hear you, Dr. Hardy. Over."

"We've lost Kapu. His radio has stopped emitting signals. We are dispatching a helicopter to the location on the Colville where he vanished. Over. Out."

Julie tried to contact Dr. Hardy several times, but he was gone.

She slipped an arm around Peter and tucked her head against his shoulder. She was giggling.

"I think we have a wolf joke out on the Colville," she said. "And I can't reach Dr. Hardy to tell him to stay where he is."

"What's up?" asked Peter.

"They tracked Kapu to the river and lost him. Wolves swim, and radios don't work underwater."

"Will it work when he comes out of the water?"

"I don't know," she said. "But we do know he is not coming straight home. I wonder why he's at the Colville."

Half an hour later the copter hung in the air above the location on the river where the radio had gone dead. Seeing no sign of wolf or collar, Kapugen landed the craft on one of the beaches, and he and

Dr. Hardy climbed out to look for wolf sign. Not far from the spot where the radio had gone dead were huge wolf prints. Trodden into the silt along the beach, the prints left the shore and went up a low embankment and out of the river valley.

"He's on his way to the Avalik den," said Kapugen. "Julie will record the meeting."

"What do you think will happen when they meet?" Dr. Hardy asked.

"Who knows?" Kapugen answered softly. "Wolves are unpredictable. What do you think?"

"I think either he will kill the new alpha or the new alpha will kill him," replied Dr. Hardy. "Alphas do not like alphas."

Kapugen chuckled. "That is true, all right," he said.

Two days later Kapu caught the scent of Willow Pup Julie and Peter Sugluk on a wind from the Avalik River. He stopped and howled his wolf name.

After a startled pause, Willow Pup Julie howled back. Kapu was not far away. She walked in his direction; he walked toward her.

They saw each other and stopped. Kapu did not come forward, so Julie made the first move. Taking slow, friendly steps, her body telling him she loved him, she came toward her friend. He hesitated. Julie dropped to her knees. He came closer, with his head turned away in mistrust. She whimpered. Slowly, slowly he brought his eyes to meet hers. His golden eyes looked steadfastly into her beautiful black eyes. He whimpered his affection for her and let her put her arms around his neck and hug him. She was family again.

Julie felt the radio collar and unsnapped it.

"You won't need this anymore," she said. Kapu shook his shoulders and head. The last of the human annoyances was gone. He spanked his front paws on the ground, his rump in the air, then got up and ran free. He was headed for the den.

Julie and Peter Sugluk could not keep up with him.

"We won't see what happens," Julie lamented as she came over a grassy rise. She stopped. Kapu stood on the highest point of land. Posed like the king he was, chest out, head up, fur glistening, he pointed his nose to the sky and howled.

"Peter," said Julie, dropping to all fours, "that's his love call to Aaka.

"Drop down, Peter. We are about to see what happens when our alpha returns to his pack."

The sun dipped toward midnight. Red and orange streaks of clouds hung across it. Julie could barely make out the silhouette of Kapu on the hill. Suddenly there were two wolves.

"Peter," Julie whispered, "it's Aaka."

The graceful pair rushed together, tails whisking, feet vaulting them into the air, bodies coming together and apart. They danced.

"No one can tell me," Peter Sugluk whispered into Julie's ear, "that wolves don't love just as we do." He kissed her cheek.

Julie straightened up. Kapu and Aaka began running—not toward the Avalik den, but toward the Upper Colville River and the empty territory there.

Rising slowly to their feet, Peter Sugluk and Julie watched Kapu and Aaka until they merged with the midnight haze and disappeared.

A wind stirred. It shook seeds from their stalks. Some seeds ballooned on the wind. Some slid down snowfields to new land, and still others dropped to earth under parent plants. For their part, Kapu and Aaka traveled on silent feet to the mountains where they in their wisdom knew they were needed.

Currently the name *Eskimo* is being replaced by *Inuit* to identify the circumpolar Eskimo people living in North America, Greenland, and Siberia. The Inuit language is a continuum of many dialects that extend across Alaska, Siberia, the Canadian Arctic, and Greenland.

There is some confusion in that it is assumed that the word *Eskimo* is a derisive word. This is not so. The native people of Alaska's North Slope call themselves Eskimos or Iñupiat Eskimos. *Iñupiaq* is an Inuit dialect and *Eskimo* is a longstanding name given to the Arctic natives by the Algonquins. It comes from "assime w," meaning "she laces a snow shoe." (The ending *t* on the word *Iñupiat* signifies the people; *q* signifies the language.)

On the west coast of Alaska the native people call themselves Yupik or Upik Eskimos, whereas in the Canadian Arctic the native people apparently prefer to be called Inuits.

Since I wrote *Julie of the Wolves* in 1972, the Iñupiat Language Commission, North Slope Borough, Barrow, Alaska, has compiled the *Iñupiaq and English Dictionary* and devised a written language. This changed the spellings of the English versions of words to reflect the true sounds of this unique dialect. In *Julie* and *Julie's Wolf Pack* I have used spellings to comply with the dictionary. I use the words *Eskimo* and *Iñupiat Eskimo* as my native friends in Barrow do to refer to themselves. *Iñupiat Eskimo* tells who you are—where you live and your cultural attributes.

Jean Craighead George